MW01248466

Table of Contents

For all the girls who dream of a tatted biker who'll steal their heart and sweep them off their feet, this one's for you.

Chapter 1

Kendall

Pain shoots through my arm as I gingerly rub my aching wrist. It isn't broken, but it sure feels like hell. My reflection in the mirror is a mess. It's tear-streaked with mascara smeared beyond recognition. I reach up and run my finger through the damp streaks under my eyes, smudging the black makeup further. A part of me almost laughs at the irony—looking as wrecked on the outside as I feel on the inside.

The worst part about dating my father's vice president of his motorcycle club? It's knowing he doesn't give a damn about what he does to me. I had thought threatening to break up with Dalton if he laid another hand on me would make him ease up a little. I was wrong. So wrong.

He yanked me by the hair, dragging me through his house as if I were nothing more than an object. My screams only seemed to fuel his fury, and he twisted my arm with such force I was certain it would break. The pain was blinding, a searing agony that stole my breath. It felt like an eternity, though it lasted only seconds, before he finally loosened his grip—maybe because my screams grew too loud, even for him to bear.

Now, I'm huddled in his bathroom, the door locked as I cry into the suffocating silence. He stormed out of the house moments ago, leaving me in this unbearable void. My father's likely on his way to the club for one of his impromptu meetings—no doubt about deals and schemes I have no say in and no desire to understand. Not that I'd ever be allowed to attend. And here I am, paralyzed by fear, unable to entertain even the thought of running. Where would I go? Anywhere I choose, they'd find me. Or worse, someone from a rival club would. Stay or leave—it doesn't matter. Either way, I'm a prisoner, caught in a nightmare with no end in sight. Not yet, anyway.

Once I scrub the smeared makeup from my face, the sting of the rough rag reminds me of the marks his hands left behind. The cold water chills my skin, but it offers a small, fleeting relief—like I'm rinsing away more than just the remnants of the day. As I towel off, my skin feels raw, and my heart continues to pound. The mirror stares back at me with a reflection I barely recognize, a stranger in my own skin.

I make my way downstairs, each creak of the floorboards echoing through the oppressive silence of the house. The faint scent of whiskey hangs in the air, his ever-present drink of choice. Without hesitation, I grab the bottle. It's become mine, too—a bitter companion and a fleeting escape from the suffocating mess my life has become.

The glass bottle feels cold against my fingers as I take a long pull, the sharp burn trailing down my throat and igniting a fire in my chest. He's already furious with me; finishing off the rest of his whiskey won't change that. I'll face his wrath later anyway, like always. Might as well give him a reason this time.

I finish off the bottle, slamming it down on the counter before hurling it at the wall. It shatters with a satisfying crash, shards flying everywhere, but it doesn't stop the burning in my chest. I'm still trapped. I stare at the broken glass scattered across the floor. Trapped because my father, the highly thought of founder of the Iron Guard Motorcycle Club, is surrounded by men just as vile as him. Men who think violence is power, and loyalty is obedience.

"Fuck!" I scream, my voice tearing through the empty house, reverberating off the walls like an accusation.

Back in Dalton's room, the scent of him clings to the sheets—whiskey, leather, and something that always makes my stomach turn. I collapse onto the bed, exhaustion pulling me under until the darkness wins.

Morning comes too soon, sunlight creeping through the blinds, and I roll over to find the bed empty. The sheets are cold, untouched. He must've stayed out all night with my father, either drinking or dealing with business. Either way, I'm thankful. At least there's a chance he'll have calmed down by the time he gets back.

In the kitchen, the warm, savory aroma of eggs and toast wafts through the air, but the stillness around me feels oppressive, pressing in like a weight I can't shake. I move on autopilot, eating each bite without tasting it, the food merely a placeholder for the emptiness gnawing at my stomach. The clock ticks on, and the silence stretches thinner and thinner. He still hasn't come home.

With a heavy sigh, I decide to head to the club. I need to figure out what my father has planned for me today, even if the thought makes my skin crawl. I slip into ripped skinny jeans that hug my legs, a black crop top that just barely reveals the rose tattoo etched over my right breast, and my scuffed, trusty Chuck Taylors. Before grabbing my keys, my fingers hover over the ink on my chest, tracing its lines—a habit, a reminder, or maybe just a way to ground myself for what's ahead.

As I step outside, the crisp morning air hits my skin, but it does nothing to soothe the unease twisting in my gut.

I slide into my silver Mustang and gun the engine, the roar echoing through the quiet morning as I peel out of the driveway. The tires screech against the pavement as I head toward downtown, the familiar streets blurring past in a haze. The wind whips through the open windows, doing little to calm the fire inside me. As I pull up to my father's club, The Sapphire, my eyes lock onto Dalton's bike parked on the side of the building, along with my father's and a few of the other guys'.

Antonio gives me a nod as I approach, his eyes flicking briefly to the bruise on my cheek but saying nothing. He opens the door for me, and I walk inside, the stale smell of beer and smoke clinging to the walls. The club won't open until later tonight, but during the day, it's all about the *real* business. Guns. Deals. Power plays. The club is just a front.

I make my way upstairs to my father's office, the familiar creak of the floorboards under my feet bringing a sense of dread I can't shake. When I push open the door, he looks up, brows furrowing as he takes in the sight of me. His expression shifts from annoyance to something resembling concern, but not quite.

"What'd you do this time?" he asks, his gaze zeroing in on my bruised cheek.

"The fuck do you care?" I snap, dropping into the chair across from his desk and propping my feet up like I own the place. I grab a lollipop from his desk and rip off the wrapper, shoving it into my mouth with more force than necessary.

"You know I care, Kendall," he sighs, leaning back in his chair. "But pissing Dalton off? That's never smart. You know how he gets when he's angry."

I roll my eyes, sucking hard on the candy as I bite back the rage bubbling under my skin. "Right. It's always *my* fault he hits me, isn't it? Like I asked for this." My voice is dripping with sarcasm as I stare at him, daring him to defend the man.

"Kendall," he says, his tone taking on that fatherly warning I've heard a thousand times. "Please, just stop being so defiant. You're only making things harder on yourself."

I let out a bitter laugh and flip him off, the lollipop clacking between my teeth. "Fuck you, Dad. Where's the woman beater anyway?"

He rubs his temples, like he's already tired of this conversation. "Counting stock in the back."

With a sigh, I get up and head downstairs, each step feeling heavier than the last. In the far back, the low hum of Dalton's voice drifts out from one of the rooms. I find him there, sifting through boxes, counting the shipment of guns that must have come in last night. Explains why he never came home and why several of the men are here this early in the day.

"Hey, babe," he says without even looking up, his attention on the inventory.

"Hey." I hop up onto an empty table, my legs swinging as I watch him, a dull ache settling in my chest. I wonder if I just walked out right now—if I made it far enough, to where no one could find me—what would he really do?

"You're on stage tonight," Dalton says casually, still not bothering to glance my way. "Wear that black lace dress I love."

Of course, not a request. Not a suggestion. Just an order. I nod, pulling out my phone and scrolling through mindless feeds, feeling a familiar hollow in my gut. I wish, just for a second, that I had the power he did. That I had a dick instead of a vagina. Then maybe I could be the one calling the shots, making others bend to my will, using their bodies to bring in money for the club.

"You got a problem with that?" Dalton's voice cuts through my thoughts, sharper now, and when I glance up, his eyes are hard, narrowing at me like I've crossed some invisible line.

"No sir," I say with forced politeness. "No problem here."

"Lose the attitude, Kendall," he snaps, slamming the lid of a crate shut with a loud clank that makes me jump. "No one wants to see a moody bitch on a pole."

I shrug, trying to keep my voice even, though the bitterness seeps through. "Then put someone else up there."

The sound of him shoving guns into containers fills the room with a metallic clatter, his frustration obvious. "Damn it, babe," he growls, finally looking at me, anger flashing in his eyes. "Why can't you just stop acting like a brat and be a good sport for once?"

"I *am* a good sport," I shoot back, hopping off the table, my voice sharper than I intend. "It's why you put me up there when your other girls call out, right? I'm always the one who shows up, no matter how fucked up things are around here."

He doesn't respond, but his glare says enough. I swallow down the urge to scream, the tight knot of anger and helplessness coiling in my stomach. It's the same damn routine, and I'm sick of playing along.

He doesn't argue. His shoulders stiffen, and he just shakes his head as he starts sorting through the delivery, organizing the guns and drugs like it's business as usual. The clink of metal and crinkling of plastic bags fill the air, a harsh reminder of what this place really is. No words, just routine, as if I'm not even here.

By the time night falls, I'm already resigned to my role. I head to the dressing room, the smell of cheap perfume and lingering sweat hitting me like a punch to the gut. My hands are steady as I slip into the tight black lace dress, the fabric clinging to me like a second skin. There's no room for modesty—this dress leaves nothing to the imagination. The built-in black bra barely does its job, and the lace straps dig into my shoulders. It stops just past my ass, and I know every inch of me is on display. I glance in the mirror and feel the usual sick twist in my stomach. This is what draws the pervy, disgusting men in. This is what keeps the club running, keeps my father in business.

The world outside thinks this is just a strip club with a bar—a little piece of sleaze in a rough part of town. But they don't know the half of it, though some assume. They don't see the guns being passed around in the back, the drugs being trafficked through the club like it's nothing. They don't know about the enemies we've made—the rival clubs, the law breathing down our necks. It's a constant threat, a life on edge, but it's all I've ever known. If I don't play along, Dalton punishes me. Hard. Most of the time, he uses his belt, the leather biting into my skin until I can barely stand. But sometimes, like last night, he uses his fists, leaving bruises that bloom ugly and dark under my skin.

I pin my hair up, a few blonde strands framing my face just right, the way Dalton likes it. My hands are steady as I cake on the makeup, thick layers to hide the bruises, my cheek still tender to the touch. I add a little extra to my eyes, making the green in them pop, even though I'd rather disappear.

Now it's just the waiting game. I sit at my dressing table, my legs spread wide as I prop my feet up, heels high and shining. My reflection stares back, vacant, my body on view for any of the guys who wander in. It's like an unspoken invitation—one I don't even want to give. But it pisses Dalton off when the other guys in the club look at me. Not because he cares about me—no, he just doesn't like sharing his toy.

The minutes crawl by until finally, three songs in, mine starts to play, 'Paint It Black' by Ciara. The beat throbs through the club, low and heavy. I stand, my six-inch heels clicking against the floor as I make my way onto the stage. The lights are dim, casting a hazy glow, and the stench of smoke and cheap whiskey fills the air. My heart pounds in time with the music as I grab the pole, my fingers curling around the cold metal. I throw my head back, wrapping a leg around it, my body moving on autopilot, all for show.

Vagina out. Legs wide. Every disgusting man in the room gets a full view, their eyes glued to me like I'm nothing more than a piece of meat. This is what I've been reduced to. This is my life.

The men in the crowd erupt into cheers, their voices a mix of whistles and howls. I'm a favorite here—always have been. I was trained for this, molded for it since I was ten, and thrown out on stage at fifteen. Every move I make, every twist of my hips and flick of my hair, draws them in closer. They can't get enough, and I know it. It's sick, but it's power.

As the bass drops, I lower myself down in front of the pole, spreading my thighs wide, offering them the view they crave. The heat of their stares is suffocating, like I'm under a magnifying glass, but I don't break. Instead, I let them drink it in. Dollar bills rain down around me, the crackle of cash hitting the stage like applause. Crawling across the floor, I gather up the bills, shoving them into my bra, the fabric stretching with each crumpled wad of money I stuff inside. The greed of it all keeps me moving.

At the center of the stage, I drop to my knees, legs spread wide again as I reach back for the pole. With a quick lift, my legs sail up over my head. My flexibility is a weapon, and I use it with precision. Every contortion, every spin is deliberate, drawing more bills from their hands. The more I make on stage, the more I get to keep, so I push harder, my muscles burning as I twirl and twist. The pole feels cool against my skin, grounding me as I spin around, letting the force of my body whip my hair through the air.

Mid-spin, my gaze lands on a man at the back of the crowd. The sea of faces fades away as his bright blue eyes lock with mine. There's no grin, no lust-fueled hunger in his expression like the others. His face is hard, unreadable, the tattoos on his neck curling up towards his jaw, adding an edge of mystery to him. His dark, messy hair falls over one eye, shadowing part of his face, and I can't tell if he's intrigued or unimpressed. He just stares—intensely.

The song ends, the final note reverberating through the room as I dismount the pole and stand, chest heaving. I bow dramatically, tossing a kiss into the crowd before strutting off the stage. The men roar their approval, some even begging for me to come back for a second round, but I won't. Once a night is my rule, and it keeps Dalton from losing his mind over the fact that too many eyes are on me for too long. He hates it. I can feel his control tightening like a noose every time I perform but my father insists on it and Dalton won't go against my father's commands.

In the dressing room, I peel off the lace dress, the fabric cool and sticky from the heat of the lights and my own sweat. My jeans and top feel like armor as I pull them on, grounding me in some twisted sense of normalcy. I shove my feet into my Chuck Taylors, lacing them up quickly before heading out to the bar.

Reggi is behind the counter tonight, grinning as I approach. "Smoking, Kendall. You were sexy as hell up there," he says, sliding a glass of whiskey towards me. The amber liquid swirls in the glass, and I toss it back in one quick gulp, the burn hitting my throat in a satisfying wave.

"Thanks, Reggi," I mutter, pulling out the wad of cash from my pocket as I slide onto a stool. The feel of the bills in my hand is both comforting and nauseating. I start counting through them. Two hundred and seventeen dollars. More than the other girls make, but none of them have been trained like me. None of them have been forced into this life since they were kids.

As I sit there, the lingering scent of sweat, whiskey, and cheap perfume clinging to me, I can't help but think about those blue eyes again, still burning in the back of my mind. Who was he? And why did it feel like he was seeing through everything I've built to survive this life?

Most of the girls here didn't start dancing until after high school, but I've been doing this for years. As I stuff the money back into my pocket, knowing my father will demand his portion of it soon enough, I hear a deep voice beside me.

"You were beautiful up there."

I turn and meet the gaze of the man whose eyes had locked with mine while I was on the pole. Those striking blue eyes up close are even more intense.

"Beautiful?" I let out a breathy laugh. Most men call me sexy, hot, or fuckable. They offer cash to take me into the bathroom for a quickie, as if that's all I'm worth. *Beautiful* isn't a word I'm used to hearing. Not even Dalton calls me that.

"You don't like being called that?" he asks, his eyes catching the light from the bulbs overhead, making the blue stand out even more.

"I can't remember the last time anyone called me beautiful," I admit, shrugging. "I'm a dancer. Men come here to see me naked, not to admire my face."

His expression shifts, almost like he's in pain, before he glances over my head. He nods to someone behind me, then leans in close, his breath warm against my ear as he whispers, "I'll see you around."

And just like that, he walks off, leaving me speechless. I blink, trying to process the interaction. What do I even say to a guy like him? Someone who almost seems to hate what this place is. His words had felt... different.

I can tell he's a biker by the leather cut slung over his broad shoulders and the way he moves with that distinct swagger—confident, deliberate, and utterly unbothered. But the patch stitched into the leather catches my eye. It's unfamiliar, unlike any of the local clubs I know. Could it be that a new motorcycle club is staking its claim in the area?

I glance back to see him standing beside another man, the two of them talking and casting occasional glances at the stage. Then he shakes his head, almost disapprovingly, before looking back at me. Our eyes meet again, and he gives me a tight-lipped smile before turning toward the exit.

As he leaves, a strange feeling settles in my chest. Men come and go through these doors, but something about him lingers. I'm not sure why, but I can't shake the thought that I might actually *want* to see him again. And that is dangerous with the eyes of my fathers men on me most of the time.

Chapter 2

Kendall

Dalton finds me at the bar later, his arm slipping around my shoulders as I finish my fourth shot of whiskey. His lips press softly against my forehead, and I close my eyes because for a moment, I can almost pretend this is what a normal relationship feels like—comfort, tenderness. If he could always be like this, life might not feel like a prison.

"You were hot as fuck up there," he murmurs, pulling me tighter against his chest, but his eyes are fixed on Dessi as she struts across the stage, her tits out for all to see. The men around us howl like wolves, their attention devouring her.

I slip out of his hold, letting his warmth fall away as I move through the crowd. Eyes track me like prey, and I can feel the weight of their hunger, the heat of their gaze burning into me. One guy reaches out, fingers brushing my ass, but someone steps in before it goes any further.

"Hands to yourself," Fletcher growls, his voice low, full of warning. The man withdraws immediately, muttering an apology.

Fletcher turns to me, his expression softening. "You really shouldn't be walking around here by yourself after being on stage."

He's right, but I shrug. Fletcher's one of the better ones—dangerous, sure, but protective in his own way. He looks out for the women, especially the ones tied to members. It's one of the few mercies around here.

"Eh, I'll be alright, but thanks." I give him a faint smile, and he pats my shoulder as I continue toward the bathrooms.

Inside, the heavy bass from the club fades into a dull throb against the walls. I lean over the sink, staring at my reflection. The bruise on my cheek is barely noticeable now, but it's there, a shadow of Dalton's rage lingering on my skin. The sight makes my stomach churn. How many times have I stood here, staring at these marks, covering them up with makeup and pretending everything's fine? Pretending *I'm* fine?

I splash water on my face, the cold shocking my senses, but it does nothing to shake the familiar numbness settling in. The bruise is easy to hide; it's the damage inside that feels impossible to cover. With a deep breath, I look away from the mirror and dry my hands, knowing that out there, it's just another performance. Another day of pretending.

When I exit the bathroom, Dalton is waiting, leaning against the wall in that shadowed alcove, his smile dark and twisted. I freeze, heart quickening as he steps forward, like a predator spotting its prey.

"Wondered where you snuck off to," he says, voice low.

"Had to pee. Is that okay?" I shoot back, my tone sharper than I intended.

He sighs dramatically, like I'm the one pushing him to the edge. "Of course it is. You make it seem like I hate you."

"Because you do?"

His lips curve into a tight smile. "No, baby. I don't." He grabs me suddenly, his mouth crushing mine in a kiss that feels more like a claim. His hands are rough, gripping my ass, pulling me against him like he owns me. "I love you, Kendall. I really do."

My breath hitches, not from the kiss but from the bitter truth hanging in the air. "You don't hit the people you love. I don't see you hitting your family, the other men, or any of the other dancers. But me? You have no problem using me to blow off steam." My voice is flat, detached. This isn't new territory—it's just another loop in the same twisted cycle. I've said these words a thousand times, but they've lost all weight, worn out by repetition.

"I'm sorry, baby." His apology is mechanical, rehearsed. He forces me down onto his lap as he takes a seat, his hands gripping tighter as he tilts my chin, kissing me again. "I'll do better, okay?"

I nod, even though I don't believe it. The hollow promise rings empty between us. It's the same as always—his words feel like smoke, vanishing before they can ever mean anything. We sit like this, locked in a make-out session as the noise of the club continues around us. The men cheer and shout, oblivious to the storm brewing in my chest, to the fracture that deepens every time Dalton swears he'll change but never does.

The night's gotten louder as the men of the club drink themselves into oblivion. The air reeks of whiskey, sweat, and testosterone as Dalton gropes me one last time before joining them in their drunken stupor. One in the morning rolls around, and I'm sitting alone in my father's office, sipping on whiskey and mindlessly scrolling through my phone, waiting for time to pass.

But it doesn't. Not really.

The roar of life outside the office, down in the club spills in through the cracks—a chaotic mix of laughter, shouts, and the pounding bass of music—but in here, the walls feel like they're closing in. The air is thick, laced with smoke and the stale stench of spilled beer. I've had enough. I've done my part—shown my face, danced just enough to be noticed—and now I want nothing more than to escape this grimy, suffocating place.

Shrugging on my leather jacket, the familiar weight gives me a small sense of comfort. I weave through the crowd, avoiding lingering stares and hands that hover too close. The cool night air greets me as I push open the door, a differentiation to the heat and chaos inside. My silver Mustang sits under the flickering glow of a parking lot lamp, its sleek body a beacon in the dimly lit lot. With quick strides, I head for it, eager to leave this place and the memories it threatens to trap me with.

The moment I step out into the parking lot, I hear a voice—deep, familiar. "You're heading out? Alone?"

I turn to see them. The two men from earlier. The one who called me beautiful stands with his arms crossed, a dark figure under the dim light, while his friend watches me with an unreadable expression.

"Seems to be that way," I reply, my tone sharp, laced with a warning. In this life, you learn fast that you have to protect yourself. I might look harmless, but the gun in my glovebox is anything but.

I step away from them, heading toward my car, the crunch of gravel under our shoes as they follow close behind. My heartbeat picks up, but I don't show it. "Can we talk?" the tattooed one asks, his voice smoother this time, like he's trying to be reasonable.

I don't stop until I reach my car, unlocking it, my fingers itching to be closer to the glovebox. When I'm sure I can grab the gun if needed, I lean back against the open door and nod at him to continue.

"We're new around here. I need some info on the Iron Guards, and I think you can provide that for me," he says, eyes cool and steady, not a hint of threat—yet.

I raise a brow, crossing my arms over my chest, which only draws more attention to the rose tattoo peeking from my shirt. His eyes flicker to it, lingering just a second too long before meeting mine again.

"You were cozy in there," he adds. "Making out with the vice president. That tells me you've got some insights."

My lips curl into a dry smirk. "Uh huh. So?" His probing makes it obvious—they're new in town, maybe a rival MC. They're fishing, trying to scope out the scene without realizing who they're talking to. Amateurs.

But the last thing I need is to be caught up in more trouble. Keeping my mouth shut seems like the safest bet.

"Just a chat on what you know about them," he presses. "Won't get back to you. Promise."

I shake my head. "I don't know anything." The lie slips out easily as I push off the car door and slide inside the vehicle, my body still tense but calm. I glance up at the two of them, neither making any move to stop me. They're not here to mess with me—at least, not yet. They're scoping the place out, just testing the waters.

If I were smart, I'd tell my father and Dalton about these guys sniffing around, but the thought of helping either of them turns my stomach. So, screw them.

I grip the steering wheel as I glance back up at the tattooed man. "If you know anything about them, walking away and never coming back is a smart move," I say coldly, my voice cutting through the night air.

With that, I slam the door shut and start the engine, the roar of the Mustang filling the silence. As I pull away, I catch a glimpse of them in my rearview mirror, standing there, talking quietly. They're planning something. I just hope I'm not around when it all goes down.

Back at my house, I pull into the garage and head straight to bed. The whiskey has me tipsy enough that a little sleep before facing Dalton outside the club sounds like a good idea.

Morning comes too soon, with my phone ringing at ten. It feels good to have slept in for once, but the sight of Dalton's name on the screen ignites a spark of anger in me. "Yeah?" I answer, stifling a yawn.

"Who were the men you were talking to last night?" he demands, his voice dripping with fury. Great.

"Which men? I spoke to dozens of them."

"Don't play stupid, Kendall. The two outside by your car. Antonio spotted you."

"Snitch," I mutter under my breath.

"Kendall!"

"I don't know, Dalton. They approached me asking what I knew about the place. I played dumb. I was tipsy and sleepy. I was going to tell you today after I woke up." It's a lie, of course. I had zero intention of telling him.

"Did they hurt you?"

Laughter bubbles up from my throat, sharp and unexpected. "No. They just asked about the club. I told them I didn't know anything and then I left. I didn't stick around for a chat. Why?"

"Because we think they shot the place up after you left." His words drain the humor from the moment, leaving me cold.

"Is everyone okay? Why didn't you call sooner?"

"Everyone is fine, babe. But can you come up here? The cops are asking for leads, and you can describe them."

"It was dark, and I didn't see them clearly, but yeah, I can come in."

"Thanks, babe. Love you."

"Mhm." I hang up and head out, still wearing the same outfit I fell asleep in, a reminder of how tangled life can get.

When I pull up to the club, a wave of dread washes over me as I spot bullet holes peppering the front wall—almost right in front of where I had parked across the lot. Fucking hell.

Stepping out of my Mustang, I spot Dalton approaching, flanked by Officer Freckles. His real name is Fred Wilks, but with his flaming red hair and a constellation of freckles covering his face, the nickname fits. He's also a corrupt piece of shit, always ready to help the MC sweep their dirty laundry under the rug.

"Kendall," Freckles greets, extending his hand. I shake it, then discreetly wipe my palm down my jeans to rid myself of the clammy sensation. Gross. "What can you tell me about the two men you spoke to last night?"

"Not much, like I told Dalton. They followed me to my car. It was dark, and I didn't think much of it since they aren't the first men to do that. They asked about the club, but I have no idea what they wanted to know. I just said I only hung out here. That's it."

"That's it?" He raises an eyebrow, his gaze probing. I can tell he's trying to read my expression, but I won't give him anything more.

"Mhm. I drove off after that."

His eyes flicker down to my chest, lingering a moment too long before darting back to my face. He turns an even deeper shade of red, and I suppress a shiver of disgust. Nasty-ass perv.

"Thanks, Kendall. Your dad is inside waiting for you." Freckles nods toward the club, signaling where I'll likely find my father. Taking a steadying breath, I leave Dalton behind with him, my steps purposeful as I head inside. Each stride tightens the knot in my stomach, bracing for the inevitable confrontation—a yelling match that's as predictable as it is exhausting.

"Kendall!" My dad's voice booms from the second floor. I look up, forcing a smile before heading to the bar.

I reach over and grab a bottle of liquor, taking a long pull straight from the neck.

"Kendall Amara!" My father's voice echoes again, more insistent this time. I take one last swig before placing the bottle back on the shelf, steeling myself for the conversation ahead as I make my way upstairs to the office.

When I walk in, he towers over me, slamming the door shut behind him. "Come on, it was just a drink," I say, feigning ignorance.

"Who were the men? Why were they asking about the club?"

"I. Don't. Know." I sink into my usual seat and pop a lollipop into my mouth. "You all keep asking, but I don't have an answer. I didn't stick around to befriend them."

"You should have come to tell me there was a new club checking us out." He settles into his chair behind the desk, his gaze piercing. His graying beard and the bags under his eyes make him look older than he actually is.

"I didn't know they were. We get plenty of men here who aren't associated with the MCs. I just assumed they were trying to hit on me, and I didn't give them a chance."

"Asking about the club while wearing cuts? Don't play coy with me, young lady." The way he says it makes me flinch.

"They didn't even know who I was. If I had thought otherwise, I would have told you. I genuinely didn't know, Dad."

He lets out a deep sigh, the tension in his shoulders sagging. "If you see them again, let me know immediately."

"Yeah, okay." I grab another lollipop from the stash he's been stocking up on since he quit smoking.

I change into my bathing suit at home and head to the lake with some friends. Dalton doesn't like me exposing my body unless I'm on stage, but I throw caution to the wind when I get the invites each summer.

As I splash around in the water with some familiar faces from school, I hear the deep rumble of motorcycles approaching. I assume Dalton has come with his men to drag me home—he likes to control everything I do—but when I turn and push my hair back, I don't recognize the bikes.

"Who are they?" Raiven asks, clinging to me from behind.

"Not sure. Guess I should go find out," I reply.

She releases her grip and steps in front of me, the water at our waists. "You don't have to. Your father can figure it out on his own."

People assume my father's MC is partly responsible for the drugs flooding the city. They're right, but there's no proof—Freckles always makes sure of that. Raiven, on the other hand, constantly worries about me getting dragged into the chaos. She's afraid I'll either end up rotting behind bars or lying in a shallow grave—just another casualty of this life. Her fears aren't misplaced, and deep down, I know she's right to be concerned.

"Just give me a sec," I tell her, walking out of the water and heading toward the group of bikers making their way down to the lake.

When I spot the tattooed man from last night, I freeze. My father's men have had plenty of shootouts, but no one has ever shot up the club. For them to do that, knowing who runs the place, they must either be reckless or incredibly dangerous.

He sees me before I can turn away, and a smile spreads across his face as his eyes quickly run up and down my body, clad in only a string bikini. "Nice seeing you again," he says, striding toward me.

"Sure it is." I watch as he tears off his shirt, messing up his already wind-whipped hair. His chest is solid stone, covered in intricate black tattoos.

A few of the other men with him strip down too, revealing swim trunks beneath their jeans. They're all handsome, adorned with tattoos and piercings.

"I'm Nolan," the man from last night says, extending his hand. He has no idea who I am; if he did, he'd be running for the hills because my father is out for blood.

Just to spite my father and Dalton, I shake Nolan's hand and introduce myself. "Kendall."

"Beautiful name." His smile brightens, and I know I should call my father to let him know they're here, but I can't resist the thrill of rebellion—it keeps the old man on his toes.

"First or last name, Nolan?" I ask flirtatiously, and the men with him chuckle as they head toward the water.

"It's my last name. What are you doing out here?"

"Swimming, getting a tan." I gesture toward my friends. "Just hanging with some pals from high school."

He nods at them, then his gaze shifts back to me. His blue eyes are piercing, and his tousled black hair partially obscures one eye, giving him an intriguing alternative vibe that I find appealing.

"Care if we join you?"

"Not at all. I'll introduce you to the girls," I say as I turn away.

He grabs my wrist and spins me around, causing my heart to race. When he notices the look of terror on my face, he immediately lets go and raises his hands.

"I was just going to say I'd rather get to know you."

"Right." I rub my wrist, hoping he doesn't notice the bruises from Dalton, but his gaze locks onto it before I can cover them up, and he snatches my arm, concern etched on his features.

"Who did this to you?" His tone turns stern, but his grip remains gentle.

"Don't worry about it," I say it harshly, hoping he'll drop the subject, but he doesn't.

"Who? And your face? What the hell?" He reaches up with his other hand and runs his thumb over my cheekbone.

I pull away from his hands and take a step back. "If you know what's best for you and your men, you'll let it go. If you were smart, you'd leave town and never come back."

"The Iron Guard's? You're protecting them?" He snarls the words, as though they leave a bad taste in his mouth.

"No. I'm protecting *you*," I reply, and he bursts into laughter.

"Beautiful, there's no need to protect me. I promise you, the Iron Guards have nothing on me."

"I doubt that. They're dangerous. Very dangerous."

Nolan leans in, his voice low as he whispers in my ear, "But I'm more dangerous, baby. I can promise you that."

A chill races down my spine at the tone of his deep, rumbling voice. "If that's the case, then I'm protecting myself."

"I wouldn't hurt you. Only those who deserve it. And I have a feeling you're more connected to them than you let on yesterday. Killian mentioned you had to be on that stage from a conversation he overheard. Then you were making out with the VP."

"Killian?"

"My buddy from last night. He can dig up any info that I need."

"Right. Well, like I said last night, I have nothing to tell you. Sorry, Nolan." I turn and head back to the water, and he returns to his men a few feet away, flirting with other girls but keeping his gaze locked on me.

"I need to go," I tell Raiven.

"That bad?" she asks, her brow furrowed.

"Yeah. I need you to do me a favor."

"Sure, anything."

"When my father and his guys show up, if they ask you about the bikers here, tell them you weren't paying attention and that I left suddenly without saying why."

"Okay, but why?"

"Because if they're smart, they'll be gone before my father shows up."

"Right, but why am I lying to your dad?"

"Can you trust me that I have a reason?"

"Of course, Kendall." She squeezes me tightly, and I head to the table, slip into my shorts, and make my way to my Mustang. Before I get in, I glance back and see Nolan still watching me. I hold his gaze for a moment before slipping into my car.

Chapter 3

Kendall

It's Sunday, which means the club is closed to outsiders. I push open the heavy doors and step inside, nodding at Meynard, who stands guard at the entrance. The familiar scent of aged wood and whiskey wraps around me as I make my way up to the office. When I enter, I find Dalton, my father, and a few other men huddled around the conference table, engaged in a serious discussion.

"Kendall," Dalton calls out, striding toward me, but I shoo him off, not wanting to deal with his overbearing attention right now.

I can feel the eyes of the men in the room lingering on me—still clad in my bikini top and shorts. It's a familiar discomfort, but I shake it off. "I saw the guys again," I tell my father, my voice steady despite the underlying concernment.

"Where?" he asks, his interest piqued as he leans forward, eyes narrowing.

"The lake," I reply, my heart racing. "I was with some girls from school when they pulled up." My pulse quickens at the thought of the bikers; I silently pray they've left before my dad's crew heads out. I glanced back at him, hoping this Nolan guy is sharp enough to recognize the warning in my gaze and knows when to cut and run.

"Did you talk to them?" he asks, standing up with wide eyes.

"No. Just saw them and headed straight here. I figured it was better not to alert them to your arrival."

"Go!" My dad roars, his command echoing through the room. The men jump to their feet, rushing out of the office. Dalton leans in to plant a quick kiss on my lips as he follows, leaving me alone with a satisfied sensation.

I head down to the bar, a smile creeping onto my face. The game I'm about to play is dangerous, but it's exhilarating. Nothing gives me more satisfaction than getting a little payback on my dad and Dalton.

After a couple of drinks, I head home and fire up my laptop, determined to dig up some dirt on this Nolan guy. He's part of another MC, and I need every scrap of info I can find to keep screwing with my dad. If I play my cards right, I can pit them against each other and get my chance to slip away unnoticed.

As I dig into Nolan's background, the details start to fall into place. Not only is he a member of an MC—Crimson Knights—but he's their president, the top leader. That explains the red knight patch on their vests. His full name is Zayne Austen Nolan, and his criminal history reads like a cautionary tale. He's been in and out of prison since he was sixteen, with a rap sheet that includes burglary, assault, attempted murder, and more offenses than I can count. The man is a walking storm of trouble.

The search doesn't reveal much beyond that. The Crimson Knights are originally from Atlanta and they seem to be settling in Houston, though I can't quite figure out why. But Nolan is about to find out the hard way that my father runs this town, and the two other MCs here are nothing compared to the influence he wields.

I make my way up to the attic, where I stash the money I've earned over the past few years into a duffle bag. Inside also sits a change of clothes, my new identity, a handgun, and burner phone ready for action. This Nolan guy may have just handed me the perfect opportunity to get out of this life.

Just as I enter the kitchen, my phone rings. I glance at the screen and see Raiven's name flash across. "Hey, how'd it go?" I ask, cracking open a beer.

"Good. The bikers left as soon as you did. Your dad took my word, and they were gone in a flash," she replies, relief evident in her voice.

"Thanks, Rai. I owe you one."

"No need. Just promise me you'll stay safe with whatever's going on."

"Of course. I love you."

"Love you too, girl."

When Thursday rolls around, Dalton pulls me aside in the club, his expression all business. "You're going on tonight in the red sequin two-piece for a bachelor party coming in." His tone is firm and demanding. Bachelor parties mean more money, and despite my reluctance to expose my body, I know I can rake in that cash. The thought is enticing as I need all the cash I can get, yet the dread lingers at the back of my mind.

Backstage, the harsh lights make the sequins on my outfit sparkle, catching the light in flashes over my chest and hips as I check my reflection in the mirror. I take a steadying breath, mentally reminding myself that this is just a performance—a way to make a living, nothing more. When my cue to come out finally signals, adrenaline surges through me. I step onto the stage, heart pounding as I climb the pole. The room dims, and the sultry music envelops me, a pulse that syncs with my own. I start spinning, letting the rhythm take over.

On the second rotation, I flip off and do the splits, feeling the rush of exhilaration. Crawling up the stage, I lock eyes with the bachelor, his expression a mix of excitement and anticipation. I rub my breasts in his face, his friends erupting into cheers, shoving cash into my bra and panties while their hands graze my skin. I can't help but revel in the attention, even as I remind myself of the boundaries I should enforce.

Spinning on my knees, I present my bare ass to him, the thin fabric of my thong barely concealing my intimacy. I shake my hips, the heat rising between my thighs as he motorboats me, laughter echoing around the room. The energy in the room is electric, yet there's a quiet unease that lingers beneath it all. I push it aside, refusing to let the discomfort take hold, focusing instead on the performance. If I let it consume me, I'll lose the drive that keeps me moving forward.

As the music shifts, I make my way back to the pole, executing a few more tantalizing moves before the song comes to an end. I bow gracefully, blowing a kiss to the bachelor as I exit the stage, the crowd still buzzing with excitement. Once in the safety of the backstage, Dalton storms in, his face flushed with anger.

"You let them touch you?" His voice is low but fierce, and I shove the crumpled bills into the pocket of my jeans that lay over my chair, the beat of the performance still coursing through me.

"Yeah. More money for me. My dad doesn't fucking care if they touch the dancers," I shoot back, my defiance fueled by the adrenaline still thrumming in my veins.

Dalton steps closer, shoving me against the wall, his breath hot against my skin. "I care. You're mine, and their hands were all over you. God, you're such a fucking whore."

I suck in a breath, anger and hurt battling within me as tears threaten to spill. "Well, if you would stand up for me, I wouldn't have to go up there."

"I can't go against your dad," he snaps, his voice tight with frustration. "But you don't have to let them touch you like a nasty skank." His hand travels up my thigh, lifting my leg over his hip, the possessiveness in his touch stirring up dread within me.

Then, without warning, he moves the fabric of my thong aside, pulling his cock out and thrusting inside me. My breath hitches, and I stare off over his shoulder, lost in a haze of confusion and anger as he fucks me against the wall with a raw intensity. The pounding of my heart matches the rhythm of his thrusts, a shambolic blend of emotions flooding my senses.

When he finally stills and pulls out, his cum drips down my thighs. I refuse to let him see me cry, quickly adjusting my thong as he tucks himself back into his jeans. His grip on my chin forces me to meet his gaze, a mix of fury and something darker dancing in his eyes.

"You're mine, bitch. Let another man touch you again, and I'll chop their fucking hands off." He pushes my head back against the wall, a final warning, before storming out of the dressing room.

Dessi and Francine rush over to me, concern etched on their faces as I slide down to my butt on the cold floor, tears streaming down my cheeks. The world feels heavy, and I can't hold back the sobs that break free. They kneel beside me trying to comfort me but it's useless when I feel so used and gross.

After what feels like an eternity, I finally pull myself together, the steadying presence of their hands guiding me through the haze of panic. I slip into my clothes from earlier, the worn fabric offering a faint sense of familiarity, a small shield against the assault still swirling in my mind. My heart is still hammering in my chest, but I take steady steps forward, each one feeling heavier than the last. As I make my way through the club, the blaring music vibrates in my bones, the laughter and chatter of the patrons almost deafening in their intensity. The weight of it all presses down on me, but I push through, my feet carrying me toward the exit as if it might offer some kind of escape from the storm inside of me.

As I reach the front doors and clear the threshold past Antonio, I can't contain myself any longer. The moment I step outside, I take off running towards my Mustang, my breath hitching as fresh tears spill down my face. Each step feels like a release, a desperate escape from the mayhem inside, as I fumble for my keys, eager to put distance between me and the pain this place causes me.

Chapter 4

Zayne

I sit at a dimly lit table, the ambient noise of the club blending with the throbbing bass, anticipation tightening my chest as I wait for Kendall to make her entrance. When she finally steps onto the stage, she's a mesmerizing sight—her confidence radiating as she flaunts her body for the group of men gathered below, but it's the one in the middle who captures her attention. He's the groom-to-be, a cocky bastard who shoves his face between her thighs, running his hands greedily over her curves.

A pang of sympathy hits me for his future wife, but it quickly dissipates as I focus on Kendall, who winks at the groom and blows a kiss before disappearing behind the curtains. Rising from my seat, I weave through the crowd, determined to catch her alone for a moment.

After she warned me to leave the lake, I did some digging and uncovered the truth. She's the daughter of Lyle Elliot, the founder and president of the Iron Guard MC. The realization stung. Kendall has been playing me for a fool, but that game ends tonight.

I'm here in Houston for business, driven by a vendetta against the IGMC. I've secured an old, rundown hotel, pouring money into its renovation to house my men. We're ready to take down these heartless bastards, and I won't let anything or anyone get in my way.

As I approach the door to the back, navigating past some of the Iron Guard's men, I take a cautious peek inside. My stomach drops as I see the VP pinning her against the wall, forcing himself inside her. I'm frozen for a moment, watching her expression shift as she seems to mentally distance herself from the encounter. The bastard finishes quickly, zipping up and leaving her there like a discarded toy.

I retreat into the shadows of the hallway as he saunters out toward the bar, a sick feeling coiling in my gut. Minutes later, Kendall steps out, her expression guarded as she makes her way through the crowd toward the front door. I take a deep breath and slip out the back exit, running around to intercept her, the thrill of the hunt coursing through my veins.

I catch up to Kendall just as she reaches her sleek silver Mustang, her breathless energy radiating off of her as she fumbles with the door. Without thinking, I push her against the car with my body, my hand clamping over her mouth to stifle any outburst. I quickly maneuver her to the other side, forcing her to sit down against the cool metal, hidden from prying eyes.

Kneeling in front of her, I can see her surprise morph into anger as tears streak down her flushed cheeks. "Are you okay?" I ask, my voice low and steady, but she only nods, the lie evident in her eyes. "Then why are you crying?" I already know the answer, but I need her to voice it, to confront it.

She pulls my hand away from her face, her gaze piercing mine. I reach out again, and she flinches, instinctively drawing back, but I don't relent. Gently, I use my thumbs to wipe the tears away, feeling the warmth of her skin against my hands.

"What happened in there?" I nod toward the club, my voice edged with concern.

"Nothing. Just ready to go home," she replies, her tone too calm, too controlled. If I hadn't just witnessed Dalton Montgomery raping her, I might have bought her words.

"Try again, Kendall Elliot."

Her eyes widen in surprise, and she shakes her head defiantly. "If you know who I am, why are you here?"

"Because I don't take lightly to men abusing and raping women."

She slaps me hard across the face before I can even process her movement. "You fucking asshole. So you saw but did nothing? Great. Want to watch it again? I can get him to go a second time with another dance."

"No, I don't like watching that shit, but there were too many of their men around for me to interfere without drawing a crowd."

"What do you want, *Zayne*?" she asks, her use of my first name catching me off guard. No one calls me by that anymore.

"So you know who I am as well. Tell me, Kendall, why was your father's man claiming you as his?"

"We're dating." The admission hangs heavy between us, her expression shifting to one of pain, and I already know the rest.

"Dating against your will, correct?"

She nods, tears threatening to spill over again, but she fights them back, batting them away with her lashes.

"Want me to handle him?"

She laughs, but I'm dead serious. "No, I don't. I'm handling it myself, so don't worry. Soon he won't be able to hurt me anymore."

"How?"

Her lips press into a thin line as she glances over my shoulder, her eyes going wide. I turn, my instincts sharpening—Killian is approaching.

He kneels beside me, assessing the situation. "They're looking for her. It won't be long before they come out here."

"You need to go home. We'll meet you there. Then we have some shit to talk about." I back off as she climbs into her car, her expression a mix of defiance and uncertainty. As she pulls away, I exchange a glance with Killian, a silent agreement hanging between us.

We follow her to her house, parking in front of the garage. The faint glow of her porch light casts a warm hue over the driveway as she unlocks the front door. We step inside and trail behind her into the kitchen, the air thick with tension.

She's either far too trusting—though I don't believe that's the case—or she's fully aware of the power she holds and knows how to use it. There's no other explanation for why a woman in her position would willingly allow two men, both dangerous and towering over her, into her home. If I had to guess, she's prepared. There are probably weapons hidden around the house, tucked away and ready to be deployed at a moment's notice. She's not as defenseless as she seems, and I think she knows exactly what she's doing.

"What do you need to talk about?" she asks, her brow furrowing slightly as her phone rings, the sound cutting through the silence like a knife.

"We're taking the Iron Guards down and could use your help from the inside," I say, meeting her gaze. The words hang in the air, heavy with implications.

She laughs, a sharp sound that surprises me. "You really think I'd want to help you two?" But there's an edge of curiosity in her voice, something that makes me think she might be more interested than she lets on.

Without missing a beat, she grabs a few bottles of beers from the fridge, popping them open with a deft flick of her wrist. "Here," she says, handing one to Killian and me before taking a long sip from her own. The phone rings again, and she glances at it with irritation, clearly not in the mood for whoever it is, though I have an idea of who is on the other line.

"Not tonight. Dalton might show up since I left early," she finally says, her eyes narrowing as she focuses back on us. "But I'll only help if you can promise that nothing I say gets back to them."

Her glare is fierce, and I can feel the weight of her words. Killian's eyes widen in surprise; he'd thought she'd refuse outright. But after what I witnessed earlier, I know she's trapped in a situation she can't easily escape.

"You got it, beautiful," I reply, my voice steady. "We'll keep it between us. You have my word."

Kendall studies us for a moment, a flicker of hope mingling with doubt in her expression. "Fine," she says, her tone softening just a fraction. "But if this blows back on me—"

"It won't," I assure her, a promise sealed with conviction. As we finish our beers, the tension in the room eases slightly, the weight of our unspoken alliance settling between us. "We'll be in touch," I say, and we head toward the door with a sense of purpose igniting within me.

Once outside, the cool night air hits us, sharp and invigorating. "You think she'll really help us?" Killian asks, his tone laced with skepticism as he tosses a leg over his bike.

"I think she wants to take them down just as much as we do," I reply, glancing back at the house. "She just needs to find her strength."

As we pull up to the hotel—now disguised as an apartment complex, stripped of any trace of its former life—I feel the weight of its transformation. The once-bustling place now stands as a reminder of our past, steeped in the darkness that brought us here. We gather with the rest of the men, the air heavy, curiosity hanging in the silence.

"Well?" Peyton slurs, his words clouded by alcohol, the familiar scent wrapping around him like a shroud. No one blames him for it; we all have our demons, and tonight, they're especially close. The shadows of that night haunt us all.

"She's in. We'll get what we need from her soon," I say, my voice steady, but it does little to ease the weight in the air. Peyton hangs his head, nodding slowly, trying to absorb what I've said.

"Thanks, Nolan. This means everything to me," he says, his voice trembling with raw emotion, the pain clear in his features.

"She was family to all of us," I remind him, placing a hand on his back. "We miss her, too, though we can't feel it as deeply as you." I pause, letting the gravity of our loss settle between us. "Lyle Elliot and his men will pay for what they did that night."

With that, I turn away, heading toward the room I've claimed as my own. I need to wash off the stench of that filthy place, to cleanse myself of the memories that cling like a second skin.

The other women who work there may do so willingly, but Kendall? She was born into this life, forced to play a role that shields her from their wrath. I hate that we have to use her, but if it means justice for Peyton, for the family we've become in this MC, I'll do whatever it takes.

The law failed us the night they crossed into our territory, tore apart our lives. Now it's our turn to settle the score, but we'll do it in a way that protects the innocent—especially the women who shouldn't be swept up in our war. But Kendall? She's a different story. I'll use her, squeeze every ounce of truth from her, until Lyle and his men are begging for mercy. And when they do, I'll have none left to give.

As the water pours over me, I let the heat clear my thoughts. I won't let my desire for vengeance cloud my judgment. This is a long game, and I'll dismantle everything they've built, brick by brick.

Once I'm clean, I towel off and stare at my reflection in the fogged mirror. My features are sharp with purpose. I've kept people at a distance, but Kendall... she's different. A complication I didn't see coming. The thought of her alone, dealing with whatever hell she's trapped in, stirs something inside me. I shouldn't care. I can't afford to.

A knock at the door pulls me from my thoughts. It's Killian, leaning against the doorframe, his face unreadable. "Peyton's a mess, man. He wants more than promises."

"He'll get his justice," I say, pulling on my shirt. "But this isn't a sprint. It's a marathon. We bleed them out slowly or risk going down with them."

Killian nods, though I can see the frustration in his eyes. He's always been the one to dive headfirst into our work. "And Kendall? What's her role in all this?" he asks with a tone I don't like.

I pause, my jaw tightening at her name. "She's our way in. The key to bringing Lyle down from the inside. Whether she knows it or not, she's the weapon we need."

"And if she turns on us?"

"Then she'll learn how dangerous it is to play both sides."

Killian studies me for a moment before shrugging. "Fine. Just don't let her get in your head. We can't afford distractions."

"I know exactly what's at stake," I snap, my tone sharper than I intended. "This ends one way—with the Iron Guard in ruins and Lyle Elliot begging for his life."

Killian slaps the doorframe before walking off, leaving me alone once more. The silence feels suffocating, wrapping around me like a vise. I run a hand through my hair, trying to shake off the doubt that's been gnawing at me ever since I saw Kendall with Dalton. I can't afford to let myself slip. Not now. Not when we're so close to the endgame.

Chapter 5

Kendall

Monday rolls around, and I'm loading my trunk with groceries for the week. As I shift a box of cereal, movement in my peripheral vision catches my attention—someone's coming too close for comfort. I twist sharply, instinctively pulling out the knife I keep tucked away, only to come face-to-face with Zayne. He stands there, completely unfazed, an amused smirk playing on his lips instead of the fear I expected.

"You scared me," I tell him, flicking the blade closed and sliding it back into my pocket.

"Sorry?" His playful tone only adds to my irritation, like he's enjoying my startled reaction.

"Couldn't you have called first? I'm sure you found my number online while snooping around," I shoot back, annoyance bubbling under the surface.

As I reach for the bag of dog food, Zayne grabs it first and places it in the open spot next to the other bags.

"You don't have a dog," he remarks, brushing off my earlier question with a nonchalant wave.

"It's for a friend," I reply, slamming the trunk closed and striding over to place the shopping basket in the corral. Zayne still lingers by my car, leaning against it with that infuriatingly smug grin plastered across his face. I cross my arms, my patience thinning. "What?" I ask, feeling more annoyed by the second as he continues to stare at me.

"You said you'd help," he replies, his tone teasing but firm.

"Ah, so you ignore what I say and expect me to be reliable? And why are you smiling?" I retort, attempting to maintain my composure.

I reach for my car door, but he beats me to it, opening it with that same stupid smile that somehow makes him even more handsome. I roll my eyes, trying to ignore the flutter in my stomach.

"I didn't call because I wasn't sure if you were alone," he explains, his eyes sparkling with mischief. "And I'm smiling because when you put the cart up, I saw the butterfly tattoo on your back."

His smile widens, and I feel an urge to reach out and slap it off his face.

"So you did hear me. Cool. And yes, I will help. Where do you want to have this conversation?" I ask, trying to sound more composed than I feel.

"Your place is fine. Meet you there." He winks before turning to walk away, leaving me standing there, flustered and frustrated. This time, I don't wait for him to make his next move; I slide into my car, shutting the door with a little more force than necessary, trying to shake off the whirlwind of emotions swirling inside me.

I pull up to Raiven's place, the morning sun casting a warm glow over the driveway. After dropping off the dog food as a thank-you for her help at the lake, I head home, my mind still buzzing from the earlier encounter. As I pull into my driveway, my heart skips a beat at the sight before me.

Zayne is already here, parked out front on his bike, the wind having whipped through his tousled hair, giving him that rugged, alpha biker look that somehow makes my pulse race. He exudes confidence, and I can't help but admire the way he leans against his bike, a picture of raw masculinity.

I've done my research. I know what he's capable of. Dangerous doesn't even begin to cover it—his rap sheet tells a story of violence and anarchy, of a man unafraid to shoot up the club to make a point.

I close the garage door after pulling in and open the front door, calling out for him to come in. I grab the bags from the trunk and carry them inside. Zayne follows me, and I'm taken aback when he helps with the groceries. His kindness throws me off balance; nothing of what I read about him suggested he had a gentle side.

Once the groceries are put away, I sit at the dining room table across from him, my fingers intertwining in a nervous gesture as I brace for the conversation ahead.

"Tell me about the club's other businesses," he prompts, his gaze steady and intense.

Deciding to play his game from earlier, I shoot back, "why'd you shoot the club up?"

"There are things about your father and his men that you probably don't know. It was a way to say we're here, to make ourselves known." His tone is matter-of-fact, as if he's recounting a mundane errand.

"You could have hurt one of the ladies or customers," I snap, anger bubbling up inside me.

"Only the Iron Guards were there. I made sure of that. We didn't fire until after they closed the doors to the public." His confidence is unnerving. I had never thought to ask about the specifics; I just assumed they'd fired without a care for the innocent bystanders. My father *and* Dalton both conveniently left that detail out.

"What do you want to know about the business?" I finally ask.

He shrugs, a playful smirk dancing on his lips. "Start by telling me what it is."

I sigh, rubbing my fingers together, trying to calm my racing heart. "They run guns and drugs."

"How?" He leans in, genuinely curious.

"Overseas. Some of the men have connections that allow them to secure deals on it all. When the other MCs get too cocky, they attack one another. My father owns this town and puts an end to any others growing too big."

Zayne laughs, but the amusement fades quickly. "Yeah, well soon, I'll own it. Do you know what they did in Atlanta a year ago?" His laughter vanishes, replaced by a serious scowl.

I think for a second before replying. "Yeah. They targeted a motorcycle club meet and secretly made deals right under the feds' noses," I reply, interpreting his expression as anger over their incursion into his territory.

"And do you know what they did afterward?" His lips thin, and he absentmindedly runs his hand over his lap, where I can see the outline of a gun tucked into his waistband.

"They went to a bar, got wasted, and then came home the next afternoon after sleeping it off," I state, recalling the details.

"Correct. Except for one missing detail that I assume they didn't tell you." His hand slows, and my heart races at the thought of what could happen if I misspeak.

"Can you stop touching your gun?" I blurt out, my voice wavering slightly.

"Observant and beautiful. You know all the signs to look out for, but you aren't included in the business, are you?"

"No, not really. My father says it's a man's job. Women are supposed to look sexy and be silent unless spoken to. I tend to push his buttons on that last part."

"I believe it," he says, a hint of admiration in his voice that sends a strange flutter through me.

The tension between us is lingering, each word a dance around the danger that lurks in every glance, every half-smile. I realize that I'm not just sitting across from a man with a dangerous past; I'm facing someone who could change everything I thought I knew about myself and my world.

"What else did they do in Atlanta?" I ask, a knot tightening in my stomach. Dad probably screwed his mom, and now Zayne's mad about it. Just another cock-measuring contest between men.

"I'll tell you, but you can't let them know that you know. It'll ruin the fun to come." His smile is haunting, a mix of charm and menace that sends chills down my spine.

"Yeah, okay. I hate them anyway, so I wouldn't tell them to begin with." My voice is firmer than I feel, but deep down, I'm anxious about the truth he's hinting at.

"That's not what I'm worried about. It's not about you ratting me out. It's you needing to verify the truth, which I can help you do, but you can't ask them at all. Not yet, at least." His words hang heavy in the air, thick with unspoken implications.

"Okay," I whisper, my heart racing as I brace for what he might reveal.

"Do you know the name Millie Teylor?" he asks, his tone shifting to something darker.

I shake my head, confusion washing over me.

"She was murdered that night in Atlanta by seven men."

A cold wave washes over me, and I swallow hard. "Was she your girlfriend?"

"No. She was married to one of my men. She was as much our family as any of my men are. She was brutally raped by seven men, beaten to a pulp, raped some more, then murdered. They left her body in the middle of the road." His voice is steady, but I can hear the underlying pain, a raw wound that has never healed.

"I—I didn't know. I swear." My head spins, disbelief coursing through me. They never mentioned this, and I thought I knew everyone they'd harmed and murdered. Maybe he's mistaken; maybe it was another club's men. "You said you have proof?"

He nods solemnly. "It gets worse, Kendall."

"What's the proof? You're positive it was my dad?"

"Yeah, it was all captured on a security camera that was lost during the investigation. I got my hands on it before it disappeared, but they wouldn't accept it afterward. Said I had altered the images. I didn't." His gaze pierces through me, filled with a desperation I can't quite understand.

My throat feels parched, and I struggle to swallow as I stare at Zayne, the weight of his words pressing down on me like a suffocating blanket. "How does it get worse?" I whisper, fear curling in my gut. I need to know if I plan to play them against each other, but the thought terrifies me.

"Your boyfriend was the main assailant." His words hang in the air like a guillotine, sharp and unforgiving. Is Dalton capable of murder? Sure. But raping and torturing an innocent woman? No way. He can't be. Or can he?

I think back to the bruises on my skin, the way he loses control. He beats me often. Will it eventually escalate to murder? Would my father let that happen? Deep down, I know he would. It would get me out of the way. If he could do that to me, he could do it to someone else.

Suddenly, I'm on my feet, the world around me blurring as I rush to the trash can. I heave, my stomach convulsing as I vomit into the container, the bitter bile burning my throat. Shakes rack my body as I collapse over the trash, tears streaming down my face. "I didn't know," I sob, the weight of my ignorance crashing down on me like a tidal wave. "I swear, I didn't know."

Is this where Zayne kills me? An eye for an eye? I stand and slowly turn, bracing for the sight of his gun leveled at me. But instead, he remains seated, watching me with a pained expression, his eyes shadowed with empathy and something deeper—something that unnerves me.

"I figured you hadn't. Not when he treats you poorly. I'm sorry this is how you had to find out. Justice failed my men. Failed Peyton. But I will not." His words hang in the air, a promise laced with intensity, and for the first time, I see the man behind the façade—the protector, the avenger.

In that moment, surrounded by the remnants of my fear and despair, I realize I'm caught between two worlds. The one that seeks to suffocate me and the one that offers a glimmer of hope, however dangerous it may be.

Chapter 6

Kendall

I'm not on stage tonight, so I skip out on the club. Instead, I find myself in a dimly lit bar a few towns over, nursing drinks to numb the anguish in my head. After Zayne dropped the truth bomb about why he's really here, I spent the rest of that day—and most of the night—combing through the case files of Millie Teylor.

The nausea hit me in waves, anger bubbling up with every word I read. The court didn't even give her husband a chance to speak. Potential witnesses were ignored. They threw the case out like Millie's life meant nothing. My father's shadow loomed over every detail, pulling strings in places I never thought possible. It became painfully clear—his reach extends far beyond this town, into the courts, into the system that's supposed to protect people like Millie.

I saved everything, stashed the evidence on a hard drive, and hid it in my bag shoved deep in the attic. Then I scrubbed my search history clean. If my father catches wind of me sniffing around, I'm as good as dead.

"Another," I mutter, my voice thick with the slur of too much whiskey. The bartender doesn't hesitate, sliding the amber liquid toward me. I take a slow sip, the burn of it filling the hollowness in my chest. On the TV above, a game between the Chiefs and Eagles plays out, the bright jerseys and roaring crowd a stark contrast to the silence that's settling inside me.

I swirl the last bit of whiskey in my glass, the world around me starting to blur at the edges. When it's empty, I lazily signal for another. But before I can even blink, a low voice growls in my ear, sending a jolt of adrenaline through my veins.

"I think that's enough for you."

I spin around, nearly falling off the stool in my drunken haze. Killian is standing there, his broad frame blocking out the bar lights. His eyes lock onto mine, the intensity in them making me bristle.

"Says who?" I slur, swaying as I try—and fail—to maintain my balance. The floor feels like it's shifting beneath me, and I grip the edge of the bar, my fingers slipping slightly on the smooth surface.

"Nolan," Killian replies gently, as if trying to keep me from tipping over.

"He's here?" My eyes dart around the bar, searching for those familiar blue eyes that always seem to draw me in, no matter how much I hate it.

Killian shakes his head, a hint of a smirk on his lips. "No, but he has me keeping an eye on you since you didn't show up at the club."

A bitter laugh escapes me. "Aww, is he worried about the daughter of the Iron Guards? How sweet." I reach out and pat Killian's cheek—harder than I mean to, but my coordination is shot. "You can tell him I can hold my own. I don't need his protection."

Killian's jaw tenses beneath my touch, his eyes narrowing. "You're drunk, Kendall. You don't even know what you need right now."

I glare at him, defiant, even though I know he's right. My head feels heavy, my vision a little too slow to catch up with the real world. The whiskey is making my thoughts fuzzy, and deep down, I know I should stop. But I don't want to. I don't want to feel anything right now—not the fear, not the anger, not the confusion swirling inside me.

"Maybe," I mutter, pulling my hand back and grabbing the next glass instead. I lift it to my lips, determined to prove my point. I'm in control—at least here, at least now.

Killian doesn't budge, his gaze steady and unmoved. "Let's go," he says, his voice firmer this time, leaving no room for argument.

I meet his eyes, wanting to challenge him, to push back, but my body betrays me. The room sways again, and my stomach flips, threatening to rebel. I squeeze my eyes shut, gripping the bar as if it'll keep me anchored.

"Fine," I mutter, defeated and sit the glass down. "But not because of you. I just don't want to puke all over this place."

He chuckles under his breath, a sound that annoys me more than it should, but I let him close out my tab and lead me out. The cold air hits me the moment we step outside, and for a second, I feel sober. The weight of everything presses down on me—the secrets, the lies, the danger lurking around every corner.

I stumble slightly, and Killian catches me, his grip firm but not rough. "Let's get you home," he says quietly.

And for the first time in a long time, I don't argue.

He climbs into the driver's seat of my car and steers us toward my place, the engine rumbling softly beneath the awkward silence. At home, he surprises me. There's no lingering expectancy or ulterior motives in his actions—Killian takes care of me as if he were an old friend, not some guy under orders to babysit me. He hands me water, sets painkillers on my nightstand, and helps me change into a tank top and shorts, all without once letting his eyes linger on my body.

It's strange. Most guys would take the opportunity to sneak a glance, but not him. His focus stays neutral, his movements careful, like he's trying to be respectful. Now I'm left wondering—is it the fact that I'm an exotic dancer that turns him off? Or is it that I'm the daughter of the rival motorcycle club, the very one that's been at the root of all the recent trouble in his life?

The question nags at me as I drift into sleep, the alcohol finally dragging me under. But when I wake up the next morning, groggy and disoriented from the hangover, those thoughts are still circling like vultures. I groan, grab the painkillers he left, and gulp them down. The dull ache in my head subsides enough for me to grab my phone from the nightstand.

A message from an unknown number flashes on the screen: *"Tell K to call me."*

I squint at the text, my lips twisting in confusion. "Good morning to you, too, Zayne," I mutter to myself, pushing off the bed. The wooden floor feels cool under my feet as I head into the living room, where Killian is sprawled across my couch, dead to the world.

I nudge him awake, and he jerks upright, blinking rapidly as if trying to remember where he is. His expression morphs into one of concern when he meets my eyes.

"Zayne says to call him. At least, I think it's Zayne," I say, holding up my phone. "I don't know the number."

Killian runs a hand over his face, trying to shake off sleep. "Yeah, it's him." His voice is low, raspy, as he pulls out his own phone and dials Zayne. I retreat to the kitchen to brew coffee, listening to the faint murmur of his conversation from the other room. The coffee pot gurgles, filling the kitchen with the rich aroma of caffeine, while Killian's voice filters through, his words vague but enough to alert me.

"Hey... Yeah, she's safe. No, he didn't... Yeah, okay. We'll see you soon."

I turn, holding a steaming mug out for him. "We?" I ask, raising an eyebrow. He takes the mug, his fingers brushing against mine briefly before he brings the cup to his lips.

"Zayne needs to talk to you," he says between sips, his face unreadable.

"Why'd you sleep on my couch?" I ask, watching him closely as he avoids my gaze. Something feels off.

He rinses his mug in the sink, the sound of running water punctuating the silence. I trail behind him, repeating my question. "Killian, why were you on my couch?"

He pauses, his back still to me, then turns around, meeting my eyes with a steady gaze. "Nolan can tell you."

I frown, irritated. "Why can't you?"

He steps closer, his voice low and serious, sending a chill down my spine. "Because it'll be best coming from him." His words hang in the air, a warning more than an answer. The weight of his tone settles over me, making my skin prickle with unease.

"Why didn't you make a move last night?" I ask before I can stop myself.

He looks at me, his gaze hardening. "Because, unlike your father and his men, I'm not a sick, perverted bastard."

His words hit me like a punch to the gut, leaving me momentarily breathless. There's something about the cold, unflinching honesty in his voice that cuts deeper than I expected.

Without another word, I retreat to my room, slipping into jeans and a leather jacket, trying to shake off the strange tension. When I return, Killian is waiting, my car keys in hand, his usual aloof expression still in place.

The drive to the hotel Zayne bought is heavy with silence, the tension thick in the air between us. The quiet hum of the engine seems to amplify every unspoken word, every lingering thought. Killian pulls into the back lot, his movements deliberate, parking the sleek silver car in the shadows where it's less likely to draw attention. The morning air is warm against my skin but the weight in my chest is anything but light. I can feel it—the unmistakable pull of something big on the horizon. Something dangerous, and yet inevitable. I don't know if I'm ready for whatever's coming, but I know I have no choice but to face it head-on.

Chapter 7

Zayne

Stepping outside in my biker vest and a pair of worn jeans, the laces of my combat boots dragging untied across the gravel. I walk up and clasp Killian's hand as he steps out of the driver's seat of Kendall's sleek, silver Mustang. The early morning sun gleams off the car's hood, but it does little to cut through the annoyance radiating from Kendall.

"What is going on?" she snaps, her tone sharp, eyes narrowing with impatience.

I give her nothing but a hard look. "Come inside," I reply, turning on my heel. I know my silence grates on her, which is exactly the point. She hates being brushed off, but she'll learn soon enough to fall in line. She has to—because she's the key to this whole operation.

Kendall will be my personal informant, whether she likes it or not. She'll plant false leads, misdirect the bastards when we need them off our scent, and when the time is right, she'll keep them distracted just long enough for us to strike. One by one, their men will fall.

The old wooden floors creak under our boots as I lead her down the narrow hall to my room, her stiff posture telling me she's wary, maybe even scared. When I close the door behind us, cutting us off from my men, she looks it too—standing by the couch, arms crossed tightly over her chest like she's trying to shield herself from something she can't control.

"Sit," I say, nodding to the couch. Her movements are slow, almost reluctant, as she lowers herself onto the cushions. I stay standing for a moment, then sit on the edge of the bed across from her, leaning forward so we're at eye level, my gaze boring into hers.

"Why did you have Killian stalking me and then stay at my house?" she asks, her voice sharp but the crack in it betrays her unease.

"Because," I say, my tone firm, "I needed to know you weren't running when you didn't show up at the club last night. You strayed from your routine. Why?"

She scoffs, the sound bitter. "Why the fuck does it matter what I do?"

"Because," I growl, leaning closer. "You promised to help me, and you can't do that if you disappear."

"I didn't disappear," she snaps back. "I wasn't needed on stage last night, so I went for a drink. Away from the club."

"Away from Dalton." I correct her, my voice darkening with the mention of him.

She nods. "Yeah."

"Has he laid his hands on you again?"

"No."

"Kendall?" I reach out, gripping her chin and forcing her to meet my gaze. Her skin is warm under my fingers, but her eyes flicker with something colder—fear, maybe, or defiance.

"He hasn't," she says, but I catch the flicker of worry deep in her eyes. She's lying to herself if she thinks it's over. Dalton's abuse won't be tempered by promises or apologies. One of these days, he'll go too far. I can see it in her eyes—she knows it, too. She knows what he did to Millie in Atlanta, and she knows she might be next.

"If he does, he's dead."

Her eyes narrow as she crosses her arms, her tone sharp. "Why do you care?"

"I don't." The words slip out too quickly, my voice a touch too hard.

Kendall's gaze holds mine for a beat too long, and her skeptical smile tugs at the corner of her lips. "Sure."

I ignore the doubt she throws my way and get straight to business. "Your first task is up. I need the names of the men who went to Atlanta with your father when Millie was murdered. There were more than seven, but I don't know exactly who all was involved."

She lifts a brow, thinking out loud. "I can ask my dad who all went with him to the meet there."

"No." My voice snaps, sharp enough to make her flinch. "If you mention it to him, he'll figure it out. He'll pin the shooting of the club on us. I can't have him knowing you're working with me. It'll put you in danger as well."

The room feels tense, her frown deepening as she processes my warning. Her fingers tighten on her arms, nails biting into her skin, but she doesn't argue. "Okay, well, it'll take time for me to gather who all went."

"Call me when you have the list." I stand, heading toward the door, but something in the air makes me stop. My hand hovers over the knob before I turn around. She's right there, inches away, close enough that I can feel the warmth radiating off her skin. Her scent—something faintly sweet, mixed with the leather of her jacket—lingers in the small space between us. I glance down at her, and for a split second, her defiance falters.

"Be careful, Kendall," I say, my voice lower, quieter now. "They'll silence you to keep their involvement under wraps."

She gives me a small nod, her expression unreadable, but I can see the weight of my words settling in. Without another word, I open the door and follow her outside, the sound of our footsteps muffled by the gravel beneath our boots. The bright sunlight casts long shadows as she walks to her car, every step measured.

I stand there, watching her as she drives away, the engine of her Mustang roaring as it disappears down the road. For a moment, I catch myself wondering why my heart beats a little too fast whenever she's around. There's something about her that unnerves me—something dangerous, maybe even tempting. But I can't afford to think about that.

Whatever the reason, I can't let it cloud my judgment. Our relationship stops at me using her for my personal gain. Once I have what I need, we'll head back to Atlanta. And she'll never see or hear from us again.

Chapter 8

Kendall

I pull up to the club just after eight the following evening. The moment I step through the doors, Dalton's angry voice hits me like a slap. "Where the fuck have you been?"

I smirk, not giving him the satisfaction of an apology. "Why? Did you miss me?"

His face twists with irritation. "No, bitch. We were hit again! I fucking called you. So did your dad."

"Hit again?" My stomach tightens at the thought. I've been ignoring phone calls so I can focus. If Zayne struck, it must've been after I left the hotel. I went home, spent hours pulling up every file I could find on the Atlanta meet last year, scribbling down the names of all the men involved. Seventeen so far, but I'm not handing anything over to Zayne until I'm sure I haven't missed anyone. And before I give him those names, he's going to do something for me.

It's time to start planning my escape from the Iron Guards. Once I leave, I'm gone for good. No coming back. My true identity will have to vanish, hidden so deep no one can ever find me again. But leaving isn't simple—I need airtight alibis, a cover for every second of my disappearance.

Dalton's voice breaks through my thoughts. "Yeah, someone shot up my fucking house," he growls, a deep frown etched into his face. "They hit while I was asleep. Thank God you weren't there."

There's a flicker of what almost looks like concern in his eyes, but I know better. Dalton doesn't care—he's suspicious. He's always suspicious.

"I was at a hotel," I say, keeping my voice casual. It's not a total lie. "Needed some space with everything going on."

He grabs my waist, yanking me closer and presses a kiss to the top of my head. The gesture feels more possessive than affectionate. "Next time, fucking tell me first."

"Yeah, okay. Sorry, Dalton." I manage to sound apologetic, even though the words taste bitter.

We walk further into the club together, but as soon as we're near the bar, Dalton heads up to the office, leaving me to my own devices. I slide onto a barstool, mentally running through the steps of my plan. There's no room for error. Not with him watching.

"Your usual?" Reggi asks, sliding a glass toward me.

"Yeah, Reg. Thanks." I take a slow sip of whiskey, letting it burn its way down. My mind drifts, but a figure sitting down beside me pulls me back. There's something familiar about him, but I can't quite place it. He orders a beer, staying quiet for a moment before leaning in close enough that I can feel his breath near my ear.

"Nolan wants to know if you have the names yet," he whispers.

Ah, that's it. I recognize him now—he was in the lobby of Zayne's hotel yesterday.

"Yes," I murmur back, keeping my tone low. "Still double-checking it."

"Good. Don't follow me or watch me leave." He stands, taking his beer with him, and disappears from my sight. I don't turn. Not until several more shots have dulled my senses enough to make me feel bold again.

Eventually, I push off the stool and head upstairs to the office. The room is empty, just as I hoped. Glancing down the hallway to make sure no one's around, I quietly close the door behind me and head straight for the filing cabinet. My father's meticulous records are inside, and I sift through them until I find what I'm looking for—files on the Atlanta meetup.

I pull out the list of attendees, my heart racing. This is it. I take a quick picture with my phone before carefully placing everything back exactly where it was. Just as I sit down at the desk, pretending to be lost in thought, the door handle jiggles. I straighten up as Fletcher walks in.

"Hey, being good up here?" he asks, his voice lighthearted, but I can sense he's watching me closely.

"Yup. Just relaxing away from the crowd," I reply smoothly.

He pats my shoulder in passing, grabbing a file off the desk. "Take care of yourself, Kendall," he says before heading out, probably to one of the meeting rooms.

I wait until it feels safe—several minutes of quiet passing—before slipping out myself. Back home, I sprawl out on my bed, pulling up the picture on my phone. The names stare back at me, identical to the ones I have written down. Seventeen men.

Ten of them either have no clue what went down or they're complicit in keeping Millie's murder buried. Either way, I've got what Zayne needs.

I call Zayne, and he picks up on the third ring. "Kendall?"

"Yeah. I have the list."

"Be there soon," he replies, cutting the call before I can even respond.

Thirty minutes later, he pulls up. We sit at the dining room table and I pull the list out of my pocket, but before handing it over, I hold it firmly in my grip, my eyes locked on him. Damn it, why does he have to look so good? That alternative style—tattoos, dark clothes, the intensity—it's all making my body betray me, every thought a distraction.

"I need something from you before I hand this over," I say, forcing my voice steady despite the thoughts running through my head.

"Name it."

"I need you to create three alibis for me. I'll let you know when I need them. They need to be solid, local, and airtight—no one should be able to poke holes in them."

He narrows his blue eyes, curiosity flickering behind them. "Why do you need an alibi?"

"If I'm helping you, you're going to help me. Can you do that?"

After a brief pause, he nods. "Yeah, I can make that happen."

I lean forward, voice firm. "If you don't keep your end of the deal, everything finds its way to my father."

His eyes widen for a split second, catching the weight of my words. "You're blackmailing me?"

"Only if I have to."

A tense silence follows, then his expression hardens. "You have my word that I'll provide three alibis." He extends his hand.

I take it, our handshake firm, sealing the deal.

I finally hand him the list. He unfolds the paper, scanning the names, and gives a slow nod as he processes what he's seeing. He doesn't say a word, but the look in his eyes tells me he knows the power we just exchanged.

"Can you do me another favor tonight?" Zayne asks, his voice low, unreadable.

I glance up, unsure. "What?"

He pulls up a video on his phone and hands it over. "It's not a pretty thing to watch, but I need to know if you can identify all seven of the men."

My stomach churns as I take his phone. A cold dread fills me, but I push play anyway, bracing myself for the horror. The screen flickers, and the scene that unfolds is worse than I could have imagined. Millie Teylor— she is stripped of her clothes, surrounded—kicked, beaten. I watch in disbelief as one by one, the men violate her, their cruelty unrelenting. Each action more brutal than the last. Dalton, front and center, egging them on with gleeful malice, joining in without hesitation.

My fingers grip the phone so tightly that I hear it creak, bile rising to my throat as Dalton raises his knife. He plunges it into Millie's chest, again and again, each stab more savage than the last. My breath catches, eyes wide with horror as she collapses, a bloodied heap, her last moments spent crawling toward the sidewalk, leaving a thick trail of blood behind her before she finally stops moving.

It feels like the world shifts. I stand abruptly, Zayne's phone slipping from my numb fingers, clattering onto the table. My vision blurs, the walls closing in as the weight of what I've just seen crushes down on me. I look around the house frantically, my chest tightening. I can't breathe.

"Kendall?" Zayne's voice sounds distant, distorted as if coming from underwater. I see him stand, concern etched across his face, but I can't focus.

I raise my hand, signaling for him to stay back. My breaths come in short gasps, and I stumble, my legs buckling beneath me. Zayne moves quickly, catching me before I hit the floor. He helps me back into the chair, his strong arms holding me up as I struggle to steady myself.

"That—Dalton did that," I whisper, my voice shaking, tears spilling down my cheeks. "He didn't even flinch." The realization settles in, cold and hard. If I stay here—if I remain under his control—Dalton will do the same to me. He's growing more violent, more dangerous with every passing day. It won't stop with beatings. He'll take my life just like he took hers.

Zayne crouches in front of me, his hand on my arm, his eyes filled with understanding. "Yeah, he did," he says quietly. "Can you identify the others? We couldn't get a clear read from the footage without knowing them firsthand. Dalton and Lyle were the only ones we could identify for sure."

I nod, sinking into Zayne's arms as my tears fall harder, my body trembling. "Lyle, Dalton, Harrison, Mike, Liam, Porter, and—and Fletcher," I choke out between sobs. My heart breaks at the last name. Fletcher. The one who was supposed to protect the women. The one who, until now, I believed to be different. How could he? How could he have stood by and taken part in something so evil, so vile?

Zayne holds me tighter, his grip firm but gentle, as if silently promising me that I'm safe for now. But nothing feels safe anymore. Not here. Not with the truth of what Dalton and the others are capable of seared into my mind.

Chapter 9

Zayne

I hold Kendall tightly against my chest as she crumbles in my arms, her sobs shaking her entire body. Any doubt I had about her involvement with her father's business is gone. The video wasn't just a test—it was a confirmation. Her reaction told me more than words ever could. It was raw, visceral, and painfully real. This woman isn't just caught up in something over her head—she is drowning in it. And now, I have the names of the men who murdered Millie.

When she finally pulls away, sitting back in her chair, I take a long look into her eyes. The fierce mask she wears—the one she uses to keep everyone at a distance—has shattered. What I see now is a girl stripped bare, all the bravado gone, leaving behind only her vulnerability. She's not the hardened woman she pretends to be. She's broken. And despite everything, I can't help but feel a tug of something deep in my chest.

"Thank you," I tell her, my voice soft. "I know being caught in the middle of all this is hell."

Her gaze is hollow as she stares back at me. No emotion, just a cold, flat surface like she's retreated somewhere deep inside herself where none of this can touch her. "You should go," she says, her voice barely a whisper, but it cuts through the air between us.

I hesitate. "You sure you'll be okay?"

"Yes." The word comes out sharp and final, but her body language betrays her. She wraps her arms tightly around herself, as if trying to hold herself together. I can't shake the feeling that if I leave now, she might fall apart all over again.

"I'll reach out when I need more of your help." It sounds colder than I intend, but there's no room for softness in this world. Not now. I head out the door, leaving her sitting alone in that cold, empty room.

Once I'm on my bike, the night air slaps me in the face, the temperature dropping fast as I speed down the road. The wind whips through my hair, biting at my skin, but I welcome the sting. It's better than the suffocating weight of everything back in that house. As the city blurs past, I let the roar of the engine drown out the thoughts that keep clawing at my mind—thoughts of Kendall, of Millie, of the twisted mess we're all caught in.

The following week, adrenaline courses through my veins as I prepare to make our next move on the club. The plan is set, and now it's just about execution. I message Kendall, instructing her through a few tasks. Moments later, she replies with a thumbs-up emoji, simple yet reassuring. Gathering my men, I go over the plan one last time.

As the clock strikes ten, we arrive at the club. The pulsating music spills out into the night, mingling with the shouts of excited patrons and the clinking of glasses. The energy is electric, the kind that sets my nerves on fire. We weave our way around to the back entrance, where Kendall waits to let us in.

When she appears, my breath catches. She's wearing a red velvet lace bra and thong set, the fabric clinging to her curves, accentuating every enticing detail. The heels strapped around her ankles elongate her legs, making her look even more alluring. She glides into the dressing room with an effortless grace, but as she moves, I can't help but steal a glance at her perfectly sculpted ass. It's a fleeting moment, but my mind races with the desire to explore every inch of her.

Kendall doesn't need the makeup she's applying at the table. She's stunningly gorgeous as she is, with a natural beauty that could light up the darkest room. Yet, I know she wears it because they make her. I've seen her without it, and the rawness of her beauty is captivating in its own right. But here, she's bound by the club's expectations, forced to adorn herself for an audience that doesn't deserve her.

The scent of hairspray fills the air, mingling with the sweet undertones of her perfume. The mixture is overwhelming. I watch her brush on the makeup, focusing on her reflection, and I feel a pang of frustration. Why does she have to do this? The thought stirs something protective within me, igniting a fire I can't ignore.

"Are you ready?" I ask, my voice low and steady, as I step closer to her. I can feel the heat radiating off her, a magnetic pull that draws me in despite the tension of the night ahead.

She meets my gaze in the mirror, her eyes a deep pool of determination. "Ready as I'll ever be." Her voice is steady, but beneath the surface, I sense the flicker of nerves.

With a final glance at her reflection, she nods, and I know we're about to step into the chaos that awaits us. Together, we're going to shake this place to its core.

My men and I blend seamlessly into the crowd, ditching our usual leather jackets and cuts for casual jeans and T-shirts that make us look like any other bar-hoppers. Eight of my loyal men flank me, each one eager for the shitstorm we're about to unleash. Tonight isn't about brute force; it's about planting the seeds of paranoia. We want the Iron Guards to sweat, to wonder who's targeting them, and to keep their heads on a swivel while they search for a phantom threat.

We've already made our mark by taking shots at the club and Dalton's house—though that last hit was personal, a little revenge for Kendall that I felt compelled to exact. I can't quite explain why I needed to do it; all I know is that it felt right.

I slip into the empty men's restroom, locking the door behind me. The small space is dimly lit, the flickering fluorescent lights casting a harsh glow over the off white walls. I pull out the bag Kendall stashed here for me, my heart racing as I get to work. I grab a can of red spray paint and let loose, writing "MURDERERS" and "DRUG DEALERS" across the stalls, mirrors, and walls. Each word is bold and deliberate, designed to draw attention. The air fills with the acrid scent of paint as I leave my mark, setting the stage for what's to come. Slowly, I'll make it clear who's behind this little disruption.

Once I'm satisfied with my handiwork, I stow the cans in the bag and step out of the restroom, my adrenaline pumping. I pass the bag to Killian, who's ready to head to the back. He slips into the area where Kendall has already cleared out the ladies, and I can hear the rattle of spray paint cans as he begins his own work of art. His artistic skills come to life as he meticulously sprays images of guns and the word "RAPISTS" across the walls of the back room. Killian's dusty art degree pays off; even in the rush of this moment, his drawings look sharp and intentional.

Once we finish up, Killian hides the bag outside the back door, and we move towards the bar. My other men are already stirring trouble, pretending to get into a drunken brawl. The loud shouts and crashing of chairs draw the attention of the entire MC, and I watch as Lyle and Dalton rush to the scene, curiosity and concern etched on their faces.

While their focus is diverted, Oliver seizes the moment. He stealthily makes his way up to the office, flanked by two of my men. In there he will tap into the security system and computer, planting his tracking devices to monitor their movements and the camera feeds. It's a crucial step in our plan, and I can't help but feel a rush of excitement at the thought of Lyle connecting everything to come.

With our tasks complete, we slip out of the bar, allowing the Iron Guards to lead out the two in a false fight. Together, we sneak around the back, hearts racing with anticipation as we make our escape. As we ride away, I can't help but chuckle to myself, feeling the thrill of the night's success. Our fun has just begun, and the Iron Guards' downfall is on the horizon.

Chapter 10

Kendall

As Zayne and his men scatter out the front door, I barely have time to catch my breath before Dalton barrels toward me, his face twisted with fury. His steps are heavy, and I can feel the weight of his anger before he even opens his mouth.

"Why the fuck did you tell the ladies to leave the dressing room?" His voice is a low growl, the kind that sends a cold chill up my spine.

"You said to," I stammer, forcing an innocent, confused expression onto my face. Though my pulse quickens in fear, I don't let him see it.

"What? When?" His hand shoots out and grabs my arm, yanking me closer to him. His grip is iron-tight, and I wince as the pain shoots up my arm. I try to pull away, but he only tightens his hold, his fingers digging into my skin until I'm blinking back tears.

"You're hurting me," I plead, voice shaking as I twist my arm, but it's no use—he's not letting go.

"I never said to leave the fucking room, Kendall." His face is inches from mine now, his breath hot and laced with the sharp scent of whiskey. His eyes burn with a mix of rage and suspicion, and for a moment, I feel like prey, cornered with nowhere to run.

"Fletch—" The words barely leave my lips before his hand swings, hard and fast. The punch echoes in my ears, and the force of it snaps my head to the side. Pain blooms across my cheek, sharp and immediate. I taste salt on my lips as the tears I've been holding back finally spill over. My face stings, and the heat from the blow spreads across my skin.

"Tell me why, bitch?" he roars, his voice reverberating in the now mostly empty club. I glance around, heart pounding in my chest as I realize the crowd has thinned out. There's no one left to witness this, no one to stop him if he decides to go further.

My mind races, and I cling to the lie, hoping it's enough to save me. "Fletcher told us you said to head to the office. We went up and waited for a while. I swear, I heard his voice through the door, Dalton," I sob, the desperation in my voice painfully real. Zayne's plan hinges on this moment, on making Fletcher look like the culprit, and I can only hope the footage shows exactly what Zayne promised. Fletcher lingering by the dressing room door, looking suspicious enough to plant a seed of doubt.

Dalton's nostrils flare as he processes my words and for a brief, terrifying second, I think he's going to hit me again. His eyes flicker with something dark and dangerous, and I brace myself for the worst.

"Fuck!" he roars, throwing me aside like I'm nothing. I stumble forward, losing my balance as my foot catches on a discarded glass. I hit the floor hard, my hands and knees scraping against the rough tile. The impact jolts through my bones, and I wince as the shards of glass cut into my palms. I press my hands against the ground, biting back the whimper that rises in my throat. Every nerve in my body is on edge, trembling with fear that he's figured out my part in this.

Dalton storms off, his boots slamming against the floor as he heads toward the stairs where my father is waiting. I watch him go, my body shaking from the adrenaline still coursing through me. My heart is pounding so hard I can hear it in my ears. Every second that passes feels like an eternity, and I'm terrified that they'll realize the truth.

When they've disappeared upstairs, I force myself to stand, my legs weak and unsteady beneath me. I limp toward the bar, feeling every cut, every bruise forming from the fall. I need something to steady my nerves, to drown out the fear that's clawing at my insides. I down a shot of whatever the bartender hands me, the burn of alcohol a welcome distraction from the pain.

But as I drive home later, the weight of what I'm doing hits me hard. I can still feel Dalton's grip on my arm, the fist that rocked me to my core. And when I'm finally alone in my room, I collapse onto my bed, burying my face in my pillow. The sobs come fast and uncontrollable, shaking my entire body as I cry into the silence.

I'm terrified. Every part of me trembles at the thought of what could happen if Dalton or my father finds out I'm involved with Zayne's plan. The memory of Millie's death flashes in my mind, brutal and seared into my thoughts. I watched it unfold in horrifying detail—Dalton's knife sinking into her flesh over and over, her screams silenced by his violence.

I could end up just like her.

The thought, that horrible possibility, keeps me up all night. No matter how much I try to calm myself, the fear tightens its grip on me. Each time I close my eyes, I see Millie. Her broken body, the look of terror on her face, and the brutal way they ended her life. Every creak in the house, every rustle of the wind against the window sends a jolt of panic through me. The dark corners of the room seem to crawl with shadows, as if someone might be lurking, waiting for the right moment to drag me away. I'm consumed by it—the gnawing terror that I'm next.

I don't know when exhaustion finally pulled me under, but when my bed shifts on the right side, my eyes snap open, and adrenaline floods my veins. Without thinking, I grab the gun from under my pillow and aim it squarely between a pair of wide, startled eyes.

"Woah!" Zayne's voice pierces the silence as he throws his hands up in surrender. "Easy there!"

"Dammit, Zayne!" I hiss, lowering the gun but keeping a firm grip on it. My heart pounds in my chest. "I could've shot you!"

He smirks, though there's a flicker of unease behind his eyes. "Yeah, didn't think of that when I snuck in here."

"Obviously." I toss the gun back under the pillow and glare at him. "Now get out so I can get dressed."

He doesn't argue. He just nods and slips out of the room, leaving me alone in the dim light of dawn creeping through the window. My pulse still races, but a strange feeling tugs at me. It's not fear. It's the thought of Zayne showing up here, unannounced, checking in on me. It stirs something deep inside—a sense of something more than the usual shit in my life.

I shove the feeling down as I get dressed, pulling on the outfit I had planned for the day. When I step into the kitchen, Zayne is waiting there, a steaming mug of coffee in his hand. He holds it out to me without a word.

I take it, but eye him warily. "What are you doing here, Zayne? If Dalton sees your bike out front—"

He chuckles, a low sound that sends a shiver down my spine. "Relax. My bike's in your garage. No one's gonna see it." His grin fades as his gaze zeroes in on my face. His eyes narrow, and in the next breath, he's fuming. "Did he hit you?" His voice is like thunder, rumbling with barely-contained rage.

I flinch at the volume of it, shrinking back a little. "Yes," I admit, my voice small. "But I'm fine. It'll heal."

His hand darts out and grabs my arm, gently but firmly. He turns it over to inspect the deep bruises in the shape of Dalton's fingers. "Oh, that motherfucker," Zayne growls, fury simmering in his tone. He looks ready to explode.

"Zayne, stop," I say, pulling my arm back, but he's not letting go easily. His thumb brushes over the bruises, a gesture that's oddly tender despite his anger. "Why do you care?" I finally ask, yanking my arm free and placing the coffee mug on the counter with a soft clink. "Why do you care what happens to me?" I run my fingers over the cuts on my hand as I stare at him.

He lets out a sharp breath, his jaw tightening. "I don't," he snaps, but the lie is written all over his face. The tension between us thickens, a crackling energy that makes it hard to breathe.

"Then why are you here?" I challenge, my voice trembling more than I'd like.

His eyes lock on mine, the storm in them barely contained. "Just checking to make sure you made it home safely. That's all."

I don't believe him, but I nod anyway. "Well, I'm fine. You can go now."

He hesitates, his gaze lingering on me like he wants to say something more. But he doesn't. Instead, he backs away slowly, the intensity of his stare never wavering until he reaches the door leading to the garage. "I'll reach out later. The fun is just beginning."

He's gone before I can respond. The garage door rises, followed by the low rumble of his bike as it comes to life. I listen to the sound fade into the distance, but the echo of his presence lingers in the air, thick and suffocating. For reasons I can't fully grasp, a part of me wishes I was riding with him. It's a reckless, dangerous thought—but there's something about Zayne that pulls me in, even when I know I should stay away.

I shake my head, trying to banish the feeling. I've spent the last year planning my escape from this hell. Zayne is just a distraction, another obstacle I can't afford. But the way he looked at me—like he was fighting his own battle of keeping his distance—it makes it harder to push him away.

I can't afford to let myself care. Not now, not ever. But I'm starting to realize that maybe, just maybe, it's already too late.

Chapter 11

Kendall

My father's voice booms through the empty club, echoing off the cold, hard surfaces like a thunderclap. The air smells faintly of stale smoke and cheap whiskey, and I can almost taste the bitter tang of sweat and anger in the space. I stand on the ground floor, my pulse quickening as I listen to him holler curses, each one sharp and venomous, reverberating off the walls like the crack of a whip.

Fletcher's gone missing, vanished after the night Zayne and his crew wreaked havoc on the club, tearing through it like a storm and tapping into the security cameras. The mess they left behind was more than physical—it's burrowed into the minds of every man in here.

Zayne told me about the all-out screaming match that erupted between my father, Dalton, and Fletcher afterward, the air thick with accusations. Fletcher held firm to his innocence, swearing up and down he had no hand in the vandalization. And he didn't. Zayne's tech man spliced the camera footage so seamlessly that Fletcher appeared to have tipped us off, sending us upstairs before someone spray painted vile words and images on the walls.

Even now, I can picture it right in my head—the perfection of the security feed, the way the footage never glitched and faltered, hiding the Crimson Knights in plain sight. Not a single shot of them or me during the chaos. Only shadows. Only silence. The aftermath was a twisted masterpiece, the walls still bearing faint traces of the red words Zayne's crew painted in fury, bleeding through the fresh coat of white paint like a wound that refuses to heal. My father rants about needing to repaint again, this time with a darker color, cursing how it'll ruin the "warmth" of the place. The warmth of a club that smells like blood and betrayal.

I bite back a laugh. It's too funny watching them all tear at each other. Dad, Dalton, the whole crew—they're suspicious of everyone now, certain their men are turning against them. Zayne's plan is working like a charm, and I'm just sitting back, watching the show, waiting for the next act to unfold.

Feigning innocence, I make my way upstairs, the worn wooden stairs creaking beneath my shoes. My heartbeat drums in my ears as I approach the office. I don't knock. I never knock. Gotta keep up the appearance that I have no clue why they're all at each other's throats.

The door swings open, and the scent of cigar smoke hits me immediately, thick and cloying. Dad is smoking again. "Am I interrupting something?" I ask, my voice casual, but I feel the weight of every gaze in the room turn on me, heavy and calculating. The tension is suffocating, but I hold my ground, my face a mask of indifference.

The bruise on my cheek burns under their stares, a dark mark against my pale skin. I can feel it throbbing with every heartbeat, a reminder of Dalton's fist from the night before last. No one mentions it, but I can tell by the way their eyes flicker over the bruise, it's not forgotten.

"No," my father says, his voice low and controlled, but there's a dark undercurrent beneath it. He's still playing his cards close, not wanting me to find out the full truth about Millie's death. But I've pieced enough together. The thought gnaws at me constantly—how her final moments were orchestrated with such cold precision. How easy it was for them. Like they'd done it before. And probably would again.

Serial rapists. Serial killers.

The men shift, the scrape of their chairs grating against the hardwood floor as they rise to leave. They nod in my direction, their eyes veiled, before filing out of the room one by one, leaving me alone with the monster who raised me.

"What's going on?" I ask, keeping my voice steady, though inside, my stomach twists into tight knots. Just standing here, looking at my father behind that desk, makes my skin crawl. His presence is oppressive, dark, like a cloud of poison seeping into every crack of the room. He's worse than I could've ever imagined. It's no wonder my mother left him. I just wish she hadn't left me behind to suffer in his world.

He doesn't answer right away, just glares at me, his eyes hard, calculating. "Business," he finally says, his voice flat. "Business that doesn't concern you."

I spot the bowl of lollipops on his desk, a sickeningly sweet reminder of my childhood. Without thinking, I grab one and pop it into my mouth. The sugary taste is almost nauseating, a contrariety to the bitterness I feel. I crinkle the wrapper in my hand, a nervous gesture I can't quite control, the sound filling the silence between us.

I shrug, meeting his cold gaze. "Fine. Don't tell me." I can't push for answers, no matter how much I want to. I can't let him suspect that I know more than I'm letting on. And I sure as hell can't ask him what he did to Fletcher, though every part of me wants to scream the question at him.

Instead, I stand there, sucking on the lollipop, pretending not to care, pretending that I'm not terrified of what he's capable of.

I take a deep breath, forcing myself to remain calm as I exit my father's office and head down to the ground floor. Each step feels deliberate, calculated, as if I'm treading on thin ice. Walking into his office and barely speaking has become part of my routine—one I've perfected over the years. Wandering around aimlessly during the day keeps suspicions at bay, a necessary survival tactic in this place. And now, more than ever, I have to keep that routine intact.

If I slip up, even just once, I could ruin everything. Zayne's entire cover could be blown if they start questioning Fletcher's innocence. But so far, none of my father's men are tech-savvy enough to even consider that someone has tapped into the cameras.

They're too busy bickering, too suspicious of each other. No one's put two and two together, they haven't even noticed that the security footage from the night of the vandalization was carefully stitched together—images spliced from different nights, different angles, all to create the perfect illusion of Fletcher outside the dressing room. It's a beautiful piece of misdirection.

As I make my way to the bar, the familiar scent of whiskey and cigarette smoke clings to the air like an old memory. The clinking of glasses and the low murmur of conversation buzz around me, but it all feels distant. Like background noise.

I slide onto a barstool, feeling the cool leather under my hands, when Dalton slumps down beside me. His presence is immediate, overbearing. The smell of booze radiates off him, even though the club hasn't opened for the public yet. His eyes are glazed, a thin film of intoxication dulling the anger I know he keeps just beneath the surface.

"Did Fletcher say anything else about why he wanted you and the other ladies to go upstairs?" His voice is slurred, each word dripping with suspicion. He's drunk, and that works in my favor. But drunk or not, Dalton's still dangerous.

I meet his gaze, keeping my expression neutral, calm. "No," I say softly, letting the lie flow as naturally as breathing. I've rehearsed this with

Zayne so many times that it feels like second nature. "I heard him through the door. He knocked twice, said that you told him to have us go upstairs and that you'd meet us there. We went without question. I figured it was a meeting about the night before we went on stage."

The words fall from my lips like silk, smooth and convincing. Inside, though, I feel a knot of tension coiling in my stomach, tightening with every passing second. Zayne's messages play over in my mind, every detail he coached me on, every line he fed me. I've practiced this speech a dozen times over the last couple of days, and now, with Dalton staring at me, it's a lifeline I'm clinging to.

Dalton narrows his eyes, his brow furrowing as if trying to pick apart my story. "Did you see anything suspicious when you were walking up to the office?"

I shake my head, keeping my voice steady. "No, Dalton. Nothing out of the ordinary. Just men drinking. No one stood out, and no one spoke to us on the way up. I'm sorry I can't be of more help."

The apology is hollow, something to fill the silence. Inside, I feel a rush of relief that my answer came out as naturally as it did. I can't afford any slip-ups, not now.

Dalton scoffs, the sound harsh and bitter. "You never were one for helping," he mutters, his words sharp and cutting. "It's why you aren't part of the *real* business. Good for bringing in men, nothing more."

His words hit harder than I expect, like a slap across the face. I watch him stand and walk off, the weight of his dismissal sinking in, leaving me cold and hollow. I sit there, feeling useless, used—exactly the way I've always felt around them.

I grip the edge of the bar, my fingers digging into the wood, fighting the familiar surge of anger and helplessness that rises inside me. The burn of Dalton's insult lingers, but I force myself to swallow it down. I can't let it show. Can't let them see how much their words still affect me, even after all these years.

The dim light above the bar casts long shadows over the bottles lined up behind it, their glass surfaces catching the light like jagged shards of broken promises. I stare at them, my mind drifting back to Zayne, to the plan we've set in motion. The plan that's working, piece by piece. And yet, I can't shake the ache that Dalton's words left behind, the bitter reminder that in my father's world, I'll never be more than a tool.

For a moment, I wonder what it would be like to leave with Zayne when he goes back home. To walk away from my father. Would Zayne protect me from my father's men? I push the thought aside, knowing it's too dangerous to dwell on. I can't afford distractions, especially not now.

Not when I'm so close to getting free.

Chapter 12

Zayne

A month has passed since the night we vandalized the Iron Guards' club. In the shadows, we've been watching them—tracking their movements, their conversations, everything they do. The paranoia has only grown within their ranks, and tonight we push it further. They're expecting a shipment of guns from Mexico, but what they'll receive is something else entirely.

We've intercepted the shipment. My men swapped out their prized weapons for toy guns, plastic replicas, and water pistols. It's a cruel joke, one designed to drive them even more insane with suspicion, to fracture their loyalty to each other. They've been walking on a tightrope of fear for weeks now, and tonight, we'll cut the rope.

Kendall hasn't needed to help much with this particular plan. That's fine by me. I've kept my distance, not wanting to draw any more attention to her than necessary. But even from afar, I make sure to check in—when I know she's alone, when it's safe to do so. A quick message here, a coded text there. It's become a silent routine between us.

Movement on the screen snaps me back to the present. My men and I sit back, eyes glued to the monitor as the semi rolls up on the screen. We watch in silence as they begin unloading the shipment into the backroom of The Sapphire. I tap my fingers lightly against the table, anticipation building in my chest. Three of my men brought the real guns here earlier, and now they sit locked in a spare room, waiting for the right moment to be put to use. For now, we just watch.

The guards at the club take their time, making sure everything seems in order. Tote after tote gets dragged into the stockroom. I can almost feel their elation through the screen, the voraciousness of a score. Then, Dalton steps forward, lifting the lid of the first tote. The look on his face is priceless—pure disbelief. He digs into the contents, rummaging through plastic rifles and neon-colored squirt guns.

He opens another tote. The same thing. And another. His face twists with frustration, then fury. Already worth it. I exchange a glance with one of my men, suppressing a grin. The rage is obvious as Dalton storms from the stockroom, his boots heavy as he marches straight to the office. The door slams against the wall as he barges in, and we watch as Lyle follows him, shouting something unintelligible. They're frantic, panicked.

They run back down to the room with the totes, tearing through them, confirming the nightmare. The once-unshakable Iron Guards are on the brink of collapse, and I get a front-row seat to the show. Their desperation bleeds through the screen as Dalton's voice rises in anger, yelling at their men, accusing them of screwing with the shipment.

Within minutes, hell erupts. Fists fly. Chairs are knocked over. The Iron Guards have turned on each other, just like we knew they would. I lean back, satisfied as I watch them unravel, their trust shattered beyond repair. It's glorious. A few well-placed words, a few calculated moves, and now the baddest, most dangerous motorcycle club in the city is crumbling under my hands.

Once the fight begins to settle, Dalton, bloodied and wild-eyed, grabs the phone. I know he's calling their supplier, scrambling to figure out how this happened, how they were played. But I'm already one step ahead. We paid off the men they use to haul shipments to keep quiet. Let him scramble. Let him drown in his own mess. The pieces are falling into place perfectly.

I push away from the screen and head to my room, a deep sense of satisfaction settling into my chest. Opening my laptop, I pull up the private feed. The screen flickers to life, showing Kendall in her bedroom, lying in bed, reading a book. She's wearing a short nightgown, her hair falling in loose waves around her face. The thin scrap of panties barely covering her only adds to the heat building inside me, but I try to focus. I didn't install these cameras to spy on her like this—but seeing her, knowing she's safe at home after Dalton's latest outburst, calms something in me.

Dalton had hit her after the vandalization at the club. He didn't suspect her of anything, but she still took the brunt of his anger. The bruises, the marks he left on her, haunt me. And no matter how much I try to keep this professional, to treat her as just another piece of the plan, I can't help the surge of attraction I feel. The way her long blonde hair falls over her shoulders, the fire in her green eyes, her feisty attitude. She drives me insane in ways I never expected.

I shake my head, cursing myself under my breath. I shouldn't be thinking about her like this. The truth is, I can't stop. Every time I see her, every time I deal with her, I get hard just thinking about what it would feel like to touch her, to have her wrapped around me. She's in my head, in my dreams at night, the reason I find release after too many sleepless hours thinking about her.

It doesn't help knowing who she really is—Lyle Elliot's daughter. She's as much a part of this world as any of them, but somehow, she feels different. She *is* different. And that only makes things more complicated.

I lean back in my chair, my hand slipping to my pants as I pull out my cock, already hard just from the thought of her. I start stroking myself, slow at first, gathering the precum at the tip as I close my eyes, imagining it's her touch on me, her soft skin beneath my hands. "Fuck," I groan, my breath hitching as the pace picks up, my mind spinning with fantasies of her tight, wet pussy wrapped around me.

I imagine the sounds she'd make, the way she'd feel beneath me, warm and soft and everything I crave but can never have.

The release comes fast, intense, and I groan as I finish, shooting into a towel I keep close for moments like this. My breath comes in ragged bursts as I lean back, trying to regain control of myself. It's wrong. I know it's wrong. But the fantasy of her keeps me sane, keeps me focused on what I need to do.

She's off-limits. She has to be, if I'm going to pull this plan off without any distractions. But for now, in the quiet of my room, I'll allow myself this one indulgence.

Tossing the towel in the hamper with the others, I climb into bed, a smile creeping across my face. The Iron Guards are probably still tearing each other apart, their club in shambles. And Kendall… she's safe. For now.

Chapter 13

Kendall

As I walk down the familiar hallway, my heart races, each step echoing in the quiet. I've been down this hall countless times since I was a child, but today feels different. The stakes are higher now. I grip the beach bag hanging from my shoulder, the knowledge of the file inside a heavy weight of what's at risk.

Entering my father's office, I hesitate for a moment, listening for any sound that might betray his approach. The silence is heavy, and my pulse quickens. I pull the file from my bag, its edges rough against my fingers, and slide it beneath a stack of papers on his desk—hidden but not buried, just like Zayne instructed.

Zayne warned me not to open it. "*It's better if you don't know,*" he'd said. I know there are things from the Vegas club meeting two years ago but that's all he would tell me. I trust Zayne. He's helping me, helping with the escape plan he doesn't even fully understand yet. He thinks it's all a distraction, a way to throw my father and Dalton off their game. Little does he know, my plans run deeper. The new car registration I've asked for this time, the paint job, the change of ownership—it's all a cover, a way to disappear once I'm ready to leave for good.

After planting the file, I give a quick thumbs-up to the camera, signaling Zayne that it's done. I try to act natural, settling into the plush chair I've claimed as mine over the years. I pop a lollipop into my mouth, feigning the usual carefree attitude I show around my father. But inside, tension coils tight in my stomach.

The door opens, and my father walks in, making my heart leap into my throat. He doesn't say anything at first, just glances at me, then at the beach bag slung beside the chair. His eyes linger for a second too long before he drops into his own chair, looking more worn out than usual. He rubs his hands through his hair, the telltale sign that he's stressed, more than I've ever seen him.

"Going to the lake today?" he asks after a beat, his voice tired.

"Yep," I respond with forced excitement, twirling the lollipop in my mouth. "Meeting Raiven there to work on my tan." The words roll easily off my tongue, though my nerves are anything but calm.

He sighs deeply, shaking his head. The lines on his face look deeper today, worry etched into every crease. Something's on his mind, something serious.

"What is it?" I ask cautiously, even though I shouldn't. But my curiosity—and maybe a part of me that still cares—pushes me to ask.

"Something's going down, and I can't figure out what or why," he admits, surprising me. He's never this candid with me about club business. It's always been a closed-off part of his life, one he shields from me. But now, it feels like a door is slightly ajar, and I can see the weight he's carrying.

"Are the girls okay?" I ask, feigning concern for the dancers while keeping my face neutral. I need to seem clueless, innocent. Every second feels like balancing on a tightrope.

"Yeah, they're fine. Don't worry about them." His words are clipped, distant.

"Okay," I reply with a shrug, grabbing another lollipop from his bowl on the desk, trying to keep the conversation light. I stand and reach for the door as I toss my bag over my shoulder, hoping to make a smooth exit before my nerves betray me or he sees the planted file.

"Kendall," my father says suddenly, his voice softer, a rare vulnerability there that stops me in my tracks. I turn my head slightly, but not enough to meet his gaze. "Be careful out there."

Without turning fully, I give him a silent thumbs-up and walk out of the room, my heart thudding against my ribs.

I don't let myself breathe until I'm halfway down the hall, the cool air of the corridor doing nothing to ease the heat flushing through me. I wonder how much longer I can keep this up—keep deceiving him, deceiving everyone. But the plan is set in motion, and there's no turning back now. Soon enough, my father won't be the only one blindsided.

The sun blazes overhead, the heat of the afternoon tempered by the cool, refreshing waves lapping at my legs. Raiven and I float lazily in the water, surrounded by our friends, laughter and conversation mixing with the soothing sounds of the beach. It's a rare moment of calm, a brief escape from the storm brewing around me. But peace never lasts long in my world.

"Kendall! Your phone's going crazy with some unknown number," Elias hollers from the shore, waving my phone in the air.

A knot tightens in my stomach wondering why Zayne is calling me so soon. I force a smile and yell back, "be right there!" I wade through the water, trying to shake off the sudden unease creeping up my spine. When I reach the shore, Elias hands me the phone just as it starts ringing again, that unknown number flashing ominously on the screen.

"Hello?" I answer, the familiar dread sinking into my bones.

"Get home now and pack a bag," Killian's voice commands, sharp and urgent. "Zayne and I are on our way, but we're out of town. We'll meet you at your place."

"What's going on?" I ask, but the anxiety in my voice goes unanswered.

"Just fucking do it, Kendall," Zayne snaps in the background, his voice strained.

"Okay, okay. I'll get dressed and—"

"Kendall," Zayne's voice cuts through, tense and foreboding, "don't let Dalton in your house."

The line goes dead before I can respond. My pulse hammers in my ears, the warning echoing in my mind. *Don't let Dalton in.*

I turn and wave frantically at Raiven, signaling that I have to go. She watches, confusion etched on her face, but I don't have time to explain. My hands are shaking as I shove my things into my bag without bothering to put on my jean shorts or shirt. Dressed in nothing but my bikini, I sprint to my car and peel out of the parking lot, the tires kicking up sand as I speed toward home.

The entire drive, my mind races, replaying Zayne's voice over and over. Something is wrong—seriously wrong. And Dalton... Dalton is a nightmare I can't afford to face right now.

When I finally reach the house, it's eerily quiet. I waste no time, running inside, I get dressed and head straight for the attic. The bag I've stashed away for emergencies feels heavier than I remember as I pull it down and sling it over my shoulder. I make my way into the kitchen where a dark figure waits in the kitchen.

Dalton.

He's leaning against the counter, arms crossed, his eyes boring into me with a hatred that chills me to my core. A slow, menacing scowl spreads across his face as he pushes himself off the counter and saunters toward me, the tension in the room thick.

"You really thought you could play a part in unraveling the club and I wouldn't find out?" His voice is low, venomous. He storms toward me, his hand grabbing my wrist with bruising force before I can reach for the gun inside of my bag.

"I-I didn't—" My words are cut short as he yanks the bag away from me and throws me across the room like I weigh nothing. My body slams into the wall, the impact knocking the wind out of me. Pain radiates through my back, and I gasp for air, scrambling to get to my feet, but Dalton is already on me. "Dalton, whatever you think I did, I didn't," I plead, but my words fall on deaf ears.

His boot slams into my stomach with brutal force, and I'm sent flying onto my back, the air rushing out of my lungs in a painful gasp. I curl up instinctively, rolling in agony as a sob escapes my throat.

"Your father hasn't figured it out yet, but I have." His voice drips with cruel satisfaction. "I've got your phone cloned, Kendall. And guess what? You forgot to delete your messages this morning with Zayne Nolan, president of the Crimson Knights."

I choke on my breath, my vision blurring as he kicks me again, harder this time. Pain explodes in my abdomen, and blood pools in my mouth. I spit it out, my body writhing in pain as I cry out for him to stop, but Dalton is far from done. He stands over me, towering like a predator toying with its prey, and places his boot on my chest and throat.

"Now it all makes sense," he sneers, pressing down hard, his weight crushing the air from my lungs. "You're fucking another club's leader. You really are a whore, Kendall."

"No," I gasp, my voice barely a whisper as I struggle to breathe. "I'm not—"

"Shut it, bitch!" he roars, pressing harder until my chest feels like it's caving in and my bones threaten to snap. "What other reason would you have for betraying your family like this?"

My fingers claw at his boot, desperate, but it's no use. The pressure is unbearable, and my vision starts to go dark. Spots dance across my eyes, and I can feel my strength slipping away, my mind on the verge of blackout. Above me, Dalton's face twists into a smirk of pure satisfaction as he watches me struggle.

The last thing I see before everything fades to black is that cruel, triumphant grin.

Chapter 14

Kendall

Just as the darkness starts to consume me, the deafening sound of my front door slamming open echoes through the house. Wood splinters as it crashes into the wall, and Dalton's furious yell fills the air, though the words are lost in my weakened state. Suddenly, the unbearable pressure on my chest vanishes, leaving me gasping for breath. My lungs burn as I suck in one desperate gulp of air after another, my vision returning in hazy fragments.

Through the blur, I see them—Killian and Zayne, the two men who have become my salvation in this moment of terror. Killian's muscular arm is wrapped around Dalton's neck, holding him in a merciless headlock that cuts off any chance of escape. Dalton thrashes like a wild animal, but Killian's grip is unyielding.

Zayne's fist connects with Dalton's gut in rapid succession—once, twice, again and again—each punch landing with a sickening thud. His face is twisted in raw fury, and the intensity of it sends a shiver through me.

"You think you can just rape, torture, and murder innocent women and get away with it?" Zayne snarls, his voice low and lethal, his words cutting through the room like a blade.

Dalton grunts, his face contorted in pain as he tries to turn away, but Zayne isn't having it. He grabs Dalton by the cheeks, fingers digging in harshly, and forces him to meet his gaze.

"It ends here," Zayne growls, his tone so chillingly cold it makes me do a double-take. Is this really the man I've come to trust? His fury is so terrifying, it feels almost inhuman. "You and your men murdered Millie Teylor, one of my men's wives, out in the street like she was nothing. We're here to repay you for that."

Dalton's body jerks as another punch lands in his stomach, this time accompanied by a squeal—like a pig caught in a trap—his voice breaking as he begs for mercy.

"Mercy?" Zayne's laugh is a dangerous mix of amusement and rage. "Where was the mercy for Millie? Where was the mercy for Annette after your little Vegas meet?" His eyes burn as he speaks, spitting each word with venom. "Where's the mercy for *Kendall*?"

The way he says my name—it's personal. His anger isn't just for the victims of Dalton's violence—it's for me. My breath catches in my throat, and my mind races at the mention of Vegas. I was right. Millie wasn't the first, and she wouldn't have been the last. My father and his men really are monsters—serial rapists, killers.

A wave of nausea hits me, and I retch, my body convulsing from the horror of it all. Nothing comes up, but the bile burns my throat. Zayne's head snaps toward me, his eyes softening for just a fraction of a second. I manage a weak, trembling smile. His attention quickly shifts back to Dalton, and without missing a beat, he drives his fist into Dalton's chest with brutal force.

Dalton's body jerks violently from the blow, and I can hear the grotesque sound of bones cracking under the relentless assault. Another punch, another sickening snap. Dalton is nearly limp now, barely able to stand. His chest heaves, struggling to keep up with the brutal pace of the beating.

"Nolan," Killian says, his voice sharp. "We don't have time to drag this out."

Zayne glances at him, then back at Dalton, whose wide, terror-filled eyes meet mine. "Lucky for you," Zayne murmurs, his tone dripping with icy finality, "your death will be quick today."

Dalton's gaze locks on mine, desperation seeping from him. "Kendall, please," he whimpers, his voice weak and trembling. The fear in his eyes is undeniable—he knows it's over.

Zayne's voice cuts through, cold and detached. "Don't worry about her. She'll be safer without you." His lip curls in disgust. "No more excuses for a man like you to beat her."

Without another word, Zayne pulls a knife from his pocket, the metallic glint catching the dim light. He flicks it open with a swift motion, and before Dalton can utter another plea, the blade plunges into his stomach. Once. Twice. Over and over, each stab more vicious than the last. Dalton's screams morph into gargled cries, his body convulsing as blood spills from his wounds.

It feels surreal, like watching a nightmare unfold before my eyes, except it's real. All too real. Dalton's gasps fade into silence, his body growing limp in Killian's hold. When Killian finally releases him, Dalton's lifeless body crumples to the floor with a sickening thud.

Zayne doesn't hesitate. He storms toward me, the bloody knife still in his hand. My heart races, my mind spinning with panic. "Please—" I stammer, my voice trembling.

Zayne's eyes flick to the knife, then back to me. Understanding dawns in his expression. Slowly, he closes the blade and pockets it. His hands, still slick with Dalton's blood, reach for my face, cradling it gently as he stares down at me, his eyes softening.

"I barely made it in time," he murmurs, his voice thick with regret. "I'm so sorry, Kendall. I was going as fast as I could to get here."

He pulls me into his arms, his embrace strong and protective. I cling to him, my body trembling as sobs wrack my chest. My eyes drift to Dalton's still form on the floor, the weight of what's just happened crashing down on me.

"I hate to break this up, but we need to get the fuck out of here," Killian says, his voice cutting through the haze of my thoughts. He holds my bag in his hand.

Zayne doesn't waste a second. He rushes me out of the house, guiding me toward a sleek black Camaro parked in the driveway. As I buckle into the passenger seat, my mind reels, struggling to process everything that's just happened.

A large green truck pulls up behind us, its engine rumbling. Killian jumps into my Mustang, ready to follow. Zayne and Killian exchange a few quick words, and then we're pulling out of the driveway, the roar of the Camaro's engine drowning out the lingering silence of the house we're leaving behind.

"We can't leave his body there," I say, my voice small as I glance back, fear gnawing at me. "They'll frame me for his murder. They'll—"

Zayne's jaw tightens, but he doesn't look at me. "In a few hours, there won't be a trace of him left. He'll just be another missing person from your father's club."

I stare out the window as the house disappears from view, trying to find solace in his words. With each passing mile, the knot of fear in my chest loosens, just a little, and I finally relax into the seat.

We pull up to the hotel-turned-apartment complex, the building looming ahead, casting long shadows in the dim light. Zayne gets out quickly, his hand resting on the small of my back as he guides me through the entrance. His men glance at us as we pass, their eyes flicking between the bloodstains on Zayne and I, as well as my rigid posture, but they say nothing. The weight of the afternoon's violence lingers in the air, unspoken. Dalton's blood feels heavy on my skin, a haunting reminder of how close I came to something far worse.

Inside his room, Zayne doesn't say much. He steps into the bathroom, turning on the shower, the sound of water breaking the silence. He gives me a nod before stepping aside, giving me space to breathe. The moment the door closes behind him, I let out a deep sigh.

The water hits my skin, warm and soothing, but it can't wash away the memory of Dalton's fingers on my arm or the sickening thud of his boots kicking me. I scrub harder, as if that will erase the bruises I know are forming. When I finally step out of the shower, I catch a glimpse of myself in the mirror. The bruises stand out in deep purples and blues, painting my chest, ribs, and stomach. My body aches, but the pain inside runs deeper.

I slip into the clothes packed in my bag, trying to shake off the heaviness clinging to me. When I step back into the room, Zayne is already sitting on the edge of his bed, freshly showered and changed into clean clothes. His black hair is still damp, hanging messily over his eyes. He looks tired, but the intensity in his gaze as he rises to his feet and approaches me makes my heart race.

He cups my face in his hands, his thumbs brushing lightly over my jaw. "Are you okay?" he asks softly, his voice filled with concern.

I swallow hard, trying to keep it together, but the lump in my throat makes it hard to speak. "No," I whisper, my voice breaking. I can feel the tears stinging behind my eyes, but I fight to hold them back. My lips tremble, betraying my strong facade.

Guilt flashes in Zayne's eyes. "I'm so sorry, Kendall. I never should've been messaging you outside of the tasks. I didn't know he'd tapped your phone as well. Whoever he used, they're good enough to not be detected. I... I failed you."

His words take me by surprise, and I tilt my head slightly, confused. "Wait, you tapped my phone too?"

He nods, his brow furrowed. "To make sure you were safe. I had to know you were okay when we weren't communicating."

"Why?" I ask, my voice barely audible.

Zayne's gaze drops to my lips before meeting my eyes again. "I don't know. I just... needed to."

The space between us seems to shrink, his breath mingling with mine as he leans closer. His lips hover just inches from mine, and for a brief minute, I lose myself in the moment, in the pull of whatever this is between us. His mouth presses softly against mine, tentative at first but quickly deepening as if we're both seeking something in the other.

Before I can fully surrender to him, the door to the room swings open.

"Shit. Sorry," Killian mutters, backing away immediately. "I should've knocked."

Zayne pulls back, retreating as if the sudden intrusion snaps him out of whatever trance we were in. He stiffens, the vulnerability vanishing in an instant, replaced by his usual guarded demeanor.

"What's up?" Zayne asks, his voice all business now.

Killian shifts awkwardly, glancing between us. "Everything's handled. Kendall's place is clean. No trace of Dalton."

I barely register their conversation. My thoughts are swirling, my heart pounding. The kiss, the way Zayne held me—it had felt so real, so genuine. But now, watching him shift so easily back into his role, it hits me. This was nothing more than a moment of weakness. A fleeting lapse. And it won't happen again.

"Yup, all good," Killian says, flashing me a quick smile.

"What is?" I ask, blinking, struggling to focus.

"Your place," Zayne answers, his voice flat. "No sign of Dalton ever being there. They'll never find his body."

"Oh. Good," I manage, feeling the weight settle back onto my shoulders. I don't ask what was done with Dalton's body. I don't want to know.

Killian leaves, and Zayne turns to me once more, his brow creased with concern. "You sure you're okay?"

"Yeah," I lie, grabbing my bag from the bathroom. But before I can take a step toward the door, Zayne stops me, his hand catching my arm.

"You don't have to go. It's not safe for you out there alone. You can take a spare room here."

"My car is outside. They'll spot it soon enough and clue them in to your hideout."

"It's already being taken care of. Tomorrow, your Mustang will belong to Rebecca Manning, just like you wanted. No one will be looking for it."

His smirk should reassure me, but instead, it deepens the ache in my chest.

"Oh," I say, forcing a smile. "Thanks."

Zayne leads me down the hall to a spare room. It's small and bare, but it's safe. As I step inside, I feel a sense of relief, but it's mixed with confusion, uncertainty. I drop my bag on the bed and glance back at him, standing in the doorway. I don't know how long I'll be here, but I realize I'm not sure if I want to leave.

Chapter 15

Zayne

I watch the live feed on my laptop, my room dimly lit by the soft glow of the screen. Lyle and several of his men are gathered in a private room, their voices low but sharp. They're discussing Dalton and Kendall's sudden disappearance, their frustration clear in every word.

"You don't think they were part of it too?" asks one of Lyle's men—a short, balding guy whose name I don't bother remembering.

Lyle's expression darkens, his jaw tightening as his fists curl at his sides. The tension in the room is growing, a storm brewing just beneath his skin. "It seems that way," he mutters, his voice low and dangerous, like the rumble of thunder before a strike of lightning. His glare could cut through steel as he continues, each word laced with venom. "My own daughter... she had access to the Vegas meet file, saw everything we did there, and then turned around and stabbed us in the back." His voice rises slightly, his fury barely contained. "She'll pay for it. I'll make damn sure of that."

The conversation drags on for over an hour, their theories spiraling into paranoia as they try to piece together what happened. They're still clueless about my involvement, but I know that won't last forever. Tomorrow night, we'll give them their first real clue—something to shake their confidence and let them know there's an outside force at play.

As the meeting finally breaks up, the club is officially closed while they investigate. The screen goes black as they shut off lights and leave the room, so I shut my laptop with a sense of finality. The weight of everything that's happened presses down on me, and I know sleep will be impossible tonight. I toss and turn, haunted by the plan I've set in motion.

At some point in the night, I find myself wandering to Kendall's room. The door creaks softly as I push it open. She's asleep, but it's far from peaceful. She twists in the sheets, her brow furrowed, soft moans escaping her lips as if she's fighting a battle even in her dreams. The bruises, both physical and emotional, are fresh, and it shows in every restless movement.

I set painkillers and a bottle of water on her nightstand, lingering for a moment as I watch her. There's something in the way she sleeps, even now, that pulls at me—a vulnerability I wasn't expecting to feel toward her. It twists in my chest, making me want to protect her, to keep her safe from everything she's been through.

I leave her room quietly and head to the lobby, sinking into a chair and flipping through the channels on the TV. The late-night talk shows provide some background noise, but my mind is far from quiet. Sleep eventually drags me under, but it's restless, filled with fragmented dreams of

Kendall, of the things I've done, and the consequences waiting just around the corner.

When I wake, the light streaming through the lobby windows tells me it's already morning. I rub my eyes and sit up, groggy, but alert enough to notice Killian standing at the coffee station with Kendall. They're talking, something casual, but the sight of them together sends a wave of jealousy crashing over me, so intense I almost gasp out loud.

I've known I was developing feelings for her, but this? This is unexpected. The tightness in my chest, the sharp sting of envy—it's more than I was prepared for.

They both turn, catching my reaction. Killian, as usual, wears a scowl, but Kendall looks... different. Relaxed, even. The strain that gripped her last night seems to have eased, and a small part of me wonders if it's because Dalton is dead. If she feels freed from the weight of him, and what that might mean for her going forward.

I push myself out of the chair and head over to them. Killian, coffee in hand, mumbles something about heading back to his room and walks away, leaving me alone with her. I sit down across from Kendall as she takes a chair at a tall table, my mind still spinning.

"How long were you and Dalton together?" I ask, needing to understand some things.

Her expression tightens, anger flashing in her eyes. "Eight years. Since I was sixteen."

The revelation makes my stomach churn. "He was an adult when you got together?" I can't hide the disgust in my voice, though it's not directed at her.

"Yes," she says softly, her voice tinged with a mix of bitterness and resignation. "He *was* ten years older than me." Her gaze drops to the floor, her fingers twitching slightly as if resisting the urge to fidget. "My father offered me to him when he took over as vice president. Dalton didn't want just a bottle of scotch as a congratulatory gift—he wanted something more... significant."

A growl rises in my throat, my hands balling into fists. "He's dead next."

Her voice is steady, but there's a sadness in it. "It's all I knew. From a young age, I was put in front of men to practice dancing, to entertain. By fifteen, I was on stage at the club for the first time."

I study her closely, my mind racing to piece together the puzzle of her life. "Where's your mother? I couldn't find much on her when I looked."

"Don't know," Kendall shrugs, her tone detached. "Dad said she left when I was four. I barely remember her. She abandoned me to live a new life."

I feel the weight of her words, the loneliness in them. "You'll never go on that stage again," I tell her, my voice firm. "You'll never use your body for money again."

For the first time since we sat down, she looks up at me, her eyes locking with mine. "I'm leaving," she says quietly, but with determination. "That's why I need the alibis, why I need the car registered under my alias."

I blink, caught off guard by her admission. "Rebecca Manning is you?"

"Yeah. I've been using you to help me escape, distracting them so I can disappear."

"Why are you telling me this?" I ask, unsure whether to be angry or impressed by her boldness.

"Because you saved me," she replies simply. "I owe you the truth."

The silence between us stretches, filled with unspoken things—regrets, plans, and emotions neither of us are fully ready to face.

"When do you plan to leave?" I ask, my voice low.

"As soon as it's safe," she says, her eyes hardening with resolve. "I can't let my father know. He can't catch wind of me once I head out either."

I sit back, studying her for a moment. This woman—so strong, yet so broken—has been plotting her escape for who knows how long. And now, as she lays her cards on the table, I find myself torn. She's been using me, sure, but she's also trusting me. And that, more than anything, makes me realize just how far I'm willing to go to keep her safe.

Because despite everything, I don't want her to leave. Not yet.

Chapter 16

Zayne

Our bikes are parked half a mile down the road, tucked behind a thick line of trees. As we make our way to the club, the night is cool, the air thick with tension. We keep to the shadows, hugging the dark corners of the road, staying out of sight. The faint hum of passing cars fills the quiet, but we're invisible to them, slipping between the pools of streetlight like ghosts. The houses we pass are mostly dark, their occupants more than likely asleep at this hour, oblivious to the shit that is about to unfold just down the road from them.

Minutes later, we arrive at the club, careful not to catch the bouncer's attention. He stands out front, scanning the lot, but we know how to avoid his gaze. The Iron Guards park their bikes on the side of the building, so we slink around the side of the building, sticking to the cover of parked cars and dumpsters. Every step feels heavy with anticipation, the weight of what we're about to do pressing down on me.

Killian is across town by now, taking Kendall with him on his bike. It gnaws at me that she's with him and not me, her arms wrapped around *his* waist on *his* bike instead of mine. But I'm needed here, to lead this part of the operation, to make sure everything goes off without a hitch. So I push the thought aside, focusing on the mission at hand.

We crouch low behind a rusted dumpster, waiting for the signal. My fingers itch with impatience, my eyes darting toward my phone every few seconds. The minutes stretch into what feels like an eternity, the silence around us thick and suffocating. Doubt starts to creep in—what if something went wrong? What if they were caught? But just as the unease settles in my gut, my phone buzzes.

"She's on the call. Several men are in the office with him," Killian's text reads.

I wave my hand to signal the others. My men move quickly, raising their handguns in unison, their faces steeled with determination. We take aim at the row of motorcycles gleaming under the faint streetlights, their chrome surfaces reflecting the faint light of the club's neon sign. The sound of the first gunshot cracks through the night, followed by several more as bullets tear into the gas tanks.

It's silent for a second—just a heartbeat of stillness—and then the explosion rips through the air. The first bike goes up in flames, the blast so sudden and violent that it sends a shockwave through the lot. The fire spreads in an instant, jumping from one bike to the next like a ravenous beast, metal twisting and groaning under the heat. The air fills with the stench of burning rubber and gasoline as the rest of the motorcycles ignite, each explosion louder than the last, until the entire lot is a blazing inferno.

The night sky lights up with the violent colors of the fire, reds and oranges flickering like fireworks. Flames shoot into the air, and the crackling of burning metal fills my ears, mingling with the shouts of the Iron Guards as they burst through the club's doors. They're too late, their eyes wide with horror as they watch their precious bikes—symbols of power and control—reduced to nothing but smoldering wreckage.

The plan works perfectly in our favor. Before they can process what's happened, we're already on the move, slipping through the shadows once again, our footsteps quick and quiet. We sprint down the road, adrenaline surging through my veins, my heart pounding in my chest. The heat from the explosion lingers on my skin, but the rush of the moment propels us forward.

We reach our bikes, hidden under the cover of darkness, and in one fluid motion, we're on them, engines roaring to life. The sound echoes into the night, but by the time anyone could think to follow us, we're already speeding down the road, the wind whipping past us as we put distance between ourselves and the destruction we've left behind.

When we reach the apartments, Kendall and Killian are already waiting. Kendall looks at me, her eyes wide with the remnants of fear, but there's something else there too—relief, maybe even admiration. I barely have time to register it before Killian steps forward, but for a moment, just a moment, I know she saw me, not just as the head of this operation, but as the man who will do anything to keep her safe.

"Mission accomplished," I say, my voice low but triumphant.

And as we gather inside, the weight of what we've done settling in, I can't help but feel a dark satisfaction. The Iron Guards won't forget this night. Their reign of fear is starting to crumble, and we're the ones who struck the first blow.

We pull up the feed on the big television in the lobby, the screen flickering to life with grainy footage from the cameras we tapped into around the club. The chaos unfolds just as we expected it to—bikes destroyed, men running in confusion, flames licking at the night sky. Lyle's voice cuts through the static, barking orders, his frustration palpable even through the speakers.

"Get those bikes put out! Someone call for backup!"

Without their motorcycles, the Iron Guards are stranded, and I can practically feel Lyle's rage boiling over as he realizes there's no way to chase us down. We made sure to stay hidden in the shadows, out of reach of their cameras, knowing exactly where their blind spots were. We won't show up on any footage. They won't have a clue who hit them. Not until they see the message left behind.

"Look at him," Killian mutters, crossing his arms as he leans against the back of the couch. "Completely losing it."

The corner of my mouth twitches into a smirk as I watch Lyle's men scramble like ants. They've never faced anything like this, so meticulously planned, so precise. But it's the grand finale I'm waiting for—the message we left behind.

On the dumpster behind the club, in bold red spray paint, the words "PAYBACK," "REVENGE," and Millie's initials "M.T." are scrawled like a bloody signature. They haven't spotted it yet, but when they do, it'll hit them like a gut punch. The Crimson Knights will be the first name that comes to their minds. It's only a matter of time before they realize they've been played, and the thought sends a dark thrill through me. Lyle will understand exactly who is behind this.

"Here it comes," Killian says, his voice low, almost gleeful. He leans in a little, eyes locked on the screen from a camera we planted as one of the Iron Guards stumbles out back, his gaze falling on the graffiti.

The man freezes, his face going pale as he stares at the message. He calls for Lyle, and the camera zooms in slightly, catching the moment Lyle steps into frame, his face a mask of fury. He reads the words, and I can practically see the gears turning in his head as he connects the dots.

"Think they'll suspect Dalton and Kendall were involved?" Killian asks, glancing at me.

"They might. And if they suspect we killed Dalton, they'll be too afraid to come looking for Kendall. Not that Lyle gives a damn about her anyway," I say, my voice cold. "Only time I've seen him even pretend to care was when he was worried she'd find out about his dirty dealings."

Lyle's face hardens on the screen, and I can see the moment he remembers what happened with Fletcher. How we framed him for the vandalization, and how he didn't hesitate to murder him in cold blood when he thought Fletcher had betrayed them. He didn't even give the man a chance to defend himself. Fletcher wasn't innocent by any means, but he sure as hell didn't turn on his club the way Lyle thought.

Now, with this new attack, I know Lyle's going to be paranoid as hell. He's going to start questioning everything and everyone around him. And that's exactly what we need him to do.

As the chaos on the screen winds down and the fire department arrives to extinguish the smoldering wreckage, I push away from the couch, glancing toward the hallway that leads to the guest rooms. Kendall disappeared to her room a while ago, and I haven't been able to shake the urge to check on her.

"I'll be back," I mutter to Killian, not waiting for his response before I head down the hall.

I find her sitting on the edge of the bed, staring at the floor, lost in her thoughts. I stand across the room for a moment, just watching her, leaning against the doorframe. Her shoulders are hunched, her hair falling in loose waves around her face, and I can see the tautness in the way she grips the edge of the mattress.

Without thinking, the words leave my mouth. "What if you came back to Atlanta with me?"

She looks up, startled, her eyes widening as she registers what I just said. "I can't." Her voice trembles as she speaks, fear lacing her words. "When my father finds out you're involved, he'll come for revenge. And if he finds me with you, he'll probably kill me himself."

She shakes slightly, her fear of Lyle so visceral that it makes my stomach twist with loathing. I hate him even more than I did before, if that's even possible.

With my voice low and resolute, I say, "he won't come looking for you, Kendall. Because when we head back home, all the Iron Guards will be dead."

She looks up at me, her eyes filled with a mix of hope and disbelief, but then a darker emotion clouds her gaze. "I can't," she says again, her voice softer this time. "Because you can barely look at me around your men. I'd be leaving here just to be put in a corner again."

Her words hit me like a slap, but I shake my head. "No corners, Kendall."

I push off the wall and walk over to her, closing the distance between us. She sits frozen as I stop in front of her, but I can see the flicker of something in her eyes—fear, yes, but also something else. Something deeper.

I reach down and gently pull her up by the arms, bringing her to her feet. She's so close now, her breath mingling with mine, her eyes searching my face as if trying to find the truth in my words. "I would never put you in a corner," I tell her, my voice low and raw.

Slowly, I inch forward, closing the space between us, my lips hovering just over hers. I can feel her breath hitch, her body trembling slightly in my grasp, but she doesn't pull away. I cup her face gently in my hands, and then, finally, I close the gap, claiming her mouth in a kiss I've been dreaming of for what feels like forever. The kiss before was a tease and I need more.

Her lips are soft and warm, and as my tongue brushes against hers, I feel a surge of need so strong it nearly overwhelms me. She moans softly into my mouth, and I swallow the sound, pulling her closer, pressing her body against mine. My arm snakes around her back, holding her tight, and for a moment, nothing else exists but her.

When I finally pull back, both of us breathing hard, I rest my forehead against hers, my voice coming out in a rough whisper. "Come back home with me."

She shakes her head, her eyes filled with conflict. "I can't…" she starts, but I see the war in her gaze—the longing, the need. She wants to say yes. She just doesn't know how to trust it.

"I'm not Dalton," I tell her softly, my thumb brushing over her cheek. "I'd never treat you like he did. Ever."

Chapter 17

Kendall

The lobby buzzes with excitement, the flashing lights from the TV reflecting off the grim faces around me. Sirens scream through the speakers, blaring louder than the distant hum of city life outside. Fire trucks, police cruisers, and ambulances swarm my father's clubhouse, their red and blue lights painting the wreckage of charred steel and melted rubber. The bikes, once symbols of power, rebellion, and freedom, now lay in ruins—gutted by flames. It's surreal to watch, but the damage is done. Those bikes, meticulously maintained and revered, won't ever run again.

"Look at them scrambling," Peyton mumbles, his voice heavy with booze. He's propped against the arm of the worn leather couch, eyes glassy, and bottle in hand.

"They know it's you now," I murmur, barely hearing myself over the footage on the screen. "What's the next step?" I yawn, exhaustion settling into my bones, not just from the sleepless nights, but from the constant unease gnawing at my chest.

When Zayne asked me to go home with him tonight in my room, I wanted to say yes. A part of me still does. But the idea scared me enough to bolt from the room. I find myself in the lobby again, pacing between the tables, caught in a battle between my mind and my heart. I've been walking a tightrope between betrayal and desire for days now.

Zayne—dangerous, lethal, calculating—feels like an enigma I can't escape. When I first agreed to help him, it was out of pure necessity, the quickest way to ensure I had an escape plan from my father's grip. But somewhere along the line, that changed. The idea of taking my father down became something real. Tangible. And Zayne's the only one I can trust to see it through.

He's not like my father, though I know he's just as dangerous. I've seen his brutality firsthand. But there's a difference. I've done my research, sifted through rumors, court records, and old newspaper clippings. He doesn't hurt women or children. Zayne's club has a code—one they call "The Avenging Angels". They don't prey on the weak; they protect them. His rap sheet is full of arrests for assault and vigilantism, saving people from abusive partners, corrupt cops, or the kind of underground filth that lives just below the surface of society. This time it just happens to be one of their own. But this kind of act has consequences. Sometimes the law doesn't care about the "why" behind your actions, just the crime. That's why he's seen the inside of a jail cell more than once.

Still, I wonder: Am I just another stray for him to save? Or is there something real between us, something deeper? I'm too afraid to ask because then I'd have to face whatever this is between us, and I'm not sure I'm ready for that. Not yet.

"Next, we start plucking these fuckers off one by one," Killian's voice pulls me back into the room. He stretches, his dark eyes gleaming with malice as he watches the panic on the TV unfold. His grin widens with every firefighter and desperate cop trying to make sense of the destruction. There's no remorse in his smile, just satisfaction, like a predator watching its prey bleed out.

I feel a shiver crawl down my spine. These men—Zayne's crew—are different from my father's. More ruthless in some ways, but somehow more honorable too. They don't strike unless they know who they're hurting. But once they do, they don't stop. This isn't just revenge; it's judgment.

And I'm not sure where that leaves me. Caught between two worlds—one I know I can't return to, and one I'm not sure I belong in.

I sit down, staring at the screen but barely seeing the wreckage anymore. My thoughts are on Zayne, the avenging angel whose cause I've tied myself to.

In my room, I stand in front of the large mirror, assessing my reflection. It's strange how everything has changed, yet on the surface, I look the same. My usual outfit—ripped jeans, a tee, and my well-worn black Chuck Taylors—couldn't be more ordinary, but today it feels like armor. I tug at the hem of my shirt, trying to focus on the task ahead, but my heart won't stop pounding. Today, I'm heading back to The Sapphire, the very place I swore I'd never return to.

The plan Zayne and I concocted feels precarious, like we're walking a tightrope above an abyss, and one wrong move could send us spiraling. I catch my own gaze in the mirror and exhale slowly. I can do this. I have to do this.

I grab my leather jacket from the bed, slinging it over my shoulders as I mentally rehearse the lies I'm about to tell. My father—cunning, suspicious, ruthless—can smell a lie from a mile away, but if I play this right, he won't even see it coming. I need to convince him that Dalton, his once-loyal enforcer, ratted him out to the Crimson Knights, setting the stage for all-out war. The truth—that Zayne's club has been solely behind the attacks all along—needs to stay buried until we've dismantled every piece of my father's empire.

And Zayne's already playing his part. He's put in a false lead with the cops, claiming insurance fraud now that the bike explosion has been reported under my father's business insurance. With a paper trail leading back to the club, the authorities will be breathing down his neck soon enough. But the real masterpiece, the true nail in the coffin, is Oliver's handiwork.

Oliver has a talent, one that feels almost otherworldly when you see him work. He's taken raw footage from security cameras—footage that shows my father outside with the bikes right before they exploded—and spliced it together with such precision that it looks like my father planned the whole thing. The brilliance of it is that it looks real, like my father sabotaged his own bikes, the very symbol of his club's power. Once this footage is "leaked," even the most loyal of his men will start to doubt him.

My job is simple, at least on paper. Convince my father that Dalton abducted me, kept me hostage in some rundown warehouse across town, and that Zayne and his men are now waiting for the next move. It's a lie wrapped in just enough truth to be believable. Dalton did disappear, but not willingly. He's crushed up with his bike somewhere, never to be seen again. Knowing my father, he'll send a few of his men to check out the warehouse, expecting to find Dalton's hideout.

What he doesn't know is that Zayne's crew will be waiting. Those men won't make it back, and when their bodies are found, the blame will fall squarely on Dalton's shoulders—and by association, his newest vice president, Satchel.

If all goes according to plan, my father will believe that Dalton and Satchel are behind the betrayal. He'll be so blinded by rage that he'll take Satchel out himself. And just like that, my father will lose several more of his men—his most trusted enforcers. One by one, his empire will crumble, just as Zayne promised.

But there's an uneasy knot in my stomach as I stand here, trying to steel myself. It's not just the plan. It's Zayne. The lines between what I'm doing for him and what I'm doing for myself have blurred.

When I first agreed to this, I was using Zayne to escape my father's grip, but now I'm not sure who's using who.

The truth is, I don't know where Zayne's protection ends and where my feelings for him begin. I've never been in a position like this—falling for someone who's every bit as dangerous as my father, but with a code that makes him seem... righteous. He fights for the innocent. He saves people. But he's still a man who walks in the shadows. And I'm about to walk even deeper into them with him.

I shake off the doubt, run my hands through my hair, and take a steadying breath. There's no room for hesitation now. Everything is in motion.

As I slip my jacket on and head for the door, the weight of the day presses down on me, but I push it aside. I have to play my part perfectly. One false move, and everything crumbles. But if we succeed, my father's reign is one step closer to ending, and I'll soon enough be free.

I reach for my phone, dialing Zayne who is already at the warehouse.

"Ready?" His voice is steady, calm.

"As I'll ever be," I reply, my voice betraying none of the nerves swirling inside me.

"Good," he says, a hint of a smile in his tone. "I'll see you on the other side, beautiful."

I hang up, my heart pounding as I step out into the hallway, the door closing behind me with a finality that feels more like the beginning of

something. Whatever comes next, there's no
turning back now.

Chapter 18

Kendall

The wind had tousled my hair by the time I reached my father's club, my shirt sticking to my back from the humidity that clung to the air. The long walk had done nothing to calm my nerves or wash away the dread pooling in my stomach. Sweat dripped down my temples, mixing with the dried streaks left from the tears I couldn't stop earlier. My face was puffy, my eyes swollen, but I wasn't about to dwell on why I had been crying—not now. Not when I was about to put this plan in motion.

As soon as I step through the front doors of The Sapphire, I can feel the shift in the room. The low murmur of conversation stops, and all eyes turn toward me. The club, dimly lit and filled with the stench of beer, smoke, and sweat, feels suffocating under their stares. It's like walking into the lion's den.

"Lyle!" Satchel's voice cuts through the silence, sharp and urgent. He's across the room in seconds, his heavy boots pounding against the floor as he grabs my arm. "Your dad is pissed," he says, tugging me toward the stairs, his grip firm and unrelenting.

I don't get a chance to respond before my father comes storming down the stairs, his face twisted in anger, fists clenched at his sides. The room stills even more, if that's possible. His presence always commands respect—or fear.

"Where the hell have you been?" he growls as he reaches me. His eyes are wild, and before I can react, he's yanking me out of Satchel's grip, shaking me hard enough that I nearly stumble.

And just like that, the tears come again—real, hot, and uncontrollable. My body wracks with sobs, and I don't even have to fake it. All the emotions I've been bottling up burst free. Every ounce of fear, guilt, and anger spills out in messy, desperate cries.

"Dalton—" I manage to choke out between sobs. "He took me to a warehouse out of town—kept me there with the Crimson Knights." The words spill out, shaky and broken, but clear enough to get my father's attention.

His grip on me tightens, his face hardening. "Dalton?" he repeats, his voice sharp and skeptical. "Why the hell would he do that?"

I can see the wheels turning in his mind, but I press on, knowing I need to sell this story perfectly. "He—he said he owed them a favor, something about wanting to take your place once you're out of the way," I sniffle, wiping at my nose, trying to look as pitiful as possible.

My father's eyes narrow, his brow furrowing deeply. "That motherfucker," he growls under his breath, the veins in his neck bulging as the anger starts to rise.

I take a shaky breath, forcing myself to meet his gaze. "There's something else I need to tell you... privately."

His eyes flash with suspicion, but he nods, jerking his head toward the stairs. "Come on," he mutters, already barking orders to his men. "Jameson, Yurik! Get up here!"

As we make our way to his office, my legs feel like lead. I can hear the thudding of my heart in my ears, louder than the stomping boots of Jameson and Yurik as they fall in line behind us. Once inside, the door shuts with a heavy thud, and I know there's no turning back now.

"What warehouse?" my father asks, his voice low and dangerous as he paces behind his desk, the familiar scent of leather and gunpowder thick in the room.

I clear my throat, hoping my voice doesn't betray me. "The big rundown brown one off Pritchett Street."

He turns sharply toward Jameson and Yurik, who stand at attention by the door. "Go scope it out. If you see Dalton, I want him brought to me alive. Take the rest of them out on sight."

The men nod and leave, and it takes everything in me not to smile. The plan is falling into place just like Zayne said it would. My father, predictable as ever, is walking straight into the trap. I know him too well. I can anticipate his every move, and today, I'm using that to my advantage.

"What do you need to tell me?" My father's voice cuts through my thoughts, bringing me back to the moment. He sits heavily in his chair, the weight of leadership and paranoia evident in the way he slouches. I pull my legs up to my chest in my usual chair across from him, wrapping my arms around them, trying to appear small, vulnerable—nervous.

"There was another man there," I whisper, rocking slightly in my chair. "He's in on it with Dalton, dad. I—I don't know how many others either."

His expression darkens, eyes narrowing as he leans forward. "Who?" he demands, his voice rising.

I glance around the room, pretending to be paranoid, then lower my voice. "Please don't tell him I told you. Dalton didn't know I escaped, but now that Satchel's seen me, he'll alert him."

"Satchel?" my father repeats, his face contorting with rage. "Are all my men turning on me?" His voice booms through the office, filled with disbelief.

"I don't know," I whisper, adding just enough fear to my tone.

He storms out of the office, his steps heavy and angry. I sit there, breathing deeply, trying to steady myself as I hear his voice rise from downstairs. The sound of his fury fills the halls, and then it gets louder, closer.

A moment later, the door flies open, and my father shoves Satchel into the room, pointing an accusing finger at him. "You were in on it? Why?"

Satchel stumbles, confusion written all over his face. "With what? Her kidnapping? The fuck I did, Lyle!" His voice is desperate, turning toward me as if I could somehow explain what was happening.

"Kendall, why are you planting this shit in his head?"

I feel a pang of guilt, deep in my gut. But it's fleeting, gone as soon as I think of what these men are capable of. They don't deserve my remorse, so I stay silent.

My father, in a fit of rage, pulls his gun from his waistband, aiming it directly at Satchel's head. Satchel freezes, his hands going up in surrender, his voice trembling as he tries to plead his case. "Lyle, wait—"

But it's too late.

The gunshot rings out, deafening in the small office. Brain matter and blood spray across the walls, across the desk, across me. I cover my mouth to stifle the scream rising in my throat as Satchel's body crumples to the floor, lifeless.

"Fuck!" my father roars, throwing the gun down onto the desk. "God damn it all!" His chest heaves with anger, his hands shaking with the aftershock of the kill. He's spiraling. I can see it in his eyes.

And all I can think is, *it's working.*

Once my father storms back downstairs, the tension in my body finally starts to unwind, if only slightly. I wait a moment, listening to the angry shouts and heavy boots thudding below, then head down the second-story hallway toward the bathroom. The fluorescent light flickers as I step in, and I catch a glimpse of myself in the mirror—blood spatters on my cheeks, remnants of Satchel's final moments. I grip the sink, staring at my reflection, my breathing heavy and erratic.

I run the water, scrubbing at my skin until the blood is gone, though the image of his lifeless body remains burned into my mind. With trembling hands, I pull out my phone and text Zayne. *'Satchel is dead. The men should be there shortly—two of them.'* My fingers hover over the screen before I hit send.

It doesn't take long before Zayne replies. *'They're gone. They'll be joining Dalton in hell. I'm on my way to get you.'*

A twisted smile pulls at my lips as I look at the mirror again. The pieces are falling into place. One by one, my father's men are being picked off, and he doesn't even realize it yet. I take a deep breath, pushing down the growing knot in my stomach, then straighten my posture. I can't fall apart. Not yet.

I wipe the last of the water from my face and head downstairs. The bar is loud, filled with the sound of clinking glasses and the deep rumble of low conversations. I sit down at one of the stools and order a whiskey, downing the first glass in one long, burning gulp. The second goes down just as fast. My head spins, but I embrace the warm, numbing sensation that settles into my bones. It dulls the ache of guilt and fear, the confusion of everything that's happening with Zayne.

After a few moments, I slip out of the bar and head toward the back, my movements carefully measured. I make my way to the dressing room and slip out the back door, knowing that with Oliver's handiwork, the security cameras won't catch a single trace of me. I'll be nothing but a ghost.

As I step out into the cool night air, I spot Zayne's bike waiting for me. Without hesitation, I throw a leg over it and wrap my arms tightly around his muscular chest. The rumble of the engine vibrates through me as he takes off, and I bury my face into his back, feeling the wind whip through my hair. There's something almost liberating about the speed, the danger, but I can't deny the fear that still lurks deep in my chest. What am I getting myself into?

We arrive at the hotel, Zayne parking his bike in one of the garages with the others. I follow him inside, my body still buzzing with adrenaline. I head straight to my room, needing a moment alone. I strip off my clothes and step into the shower, letting the hot water wash away the sweat, the blood in my hair, and the guilt that clings to me. But the water does nothing to cleanse the emotional weight I'm carrying.

By the time I step out, my body wrapped in a towel, my face is once again swollen from crying. I catch my reflection in the fogged-up mirror, the sight of myself looking so small and broken twisting my stomach into knots. Before I can lose myself in my thoughts, I hear a knock at the door. My breath catches when I see Zayne leaning casually against the wall as I exit the bathroom, watching me with an intensity that makes my heart pound.

He saunters over, his presence filling the room as if it were his to command. I instinctively wrap my arms around myself, holding the towel tighter, but his eyes are locked on mine, burning with something between desire and concern. His jaw is tense, his lips pressed into a thin line as he steps closer. I can feel the heat radiating off his body, the way his gaze traces the lines of my face, down to my trembling lips.

He doesn't hesitate when he reaches for me, cupping my face in his hands. His touch is both gentle and firm, and I can see the questions in his eyes. "You were crying in there. Why?" His voice is low, rough, like he's trying to keep himself under control.

I swallow hard, the vulnerability of the moment crashing down on me. I've kept so much hidden from him—things I didn't even admit to myself. I should lie. I should protect myself from him, but the truth spills out before I can stop it. "Because..." My voice falters, and I close my eyes, my chest tightening painfully. "Because I'm falling for you, and it's going to hurt like hell when I leave."

There. I said it. The words hang heavy in the air, and for a moment, the room feels impossibly still. My heart races, and I can barely breathe as I wait for his response.

Zayne's grip on my face tightens ever so slightly, his forehead leaning down to press against mine. "Kendall," he whispers, his voice strained.

The weight of my admission hits him, and something shifts in his expression. His eyes soften, and before I know it, his lips are on mine. The kiss is gentle, so unlike the storm of emotions swirling between us.

His lips move against mine with tenderness, his breath mingling with mine as he whispers, "I've fallen for you, too."

His words make my heart clench, and for a moment, I melt into the kiss, allowing myself to feel everything I've been holding back. His hands slide down to my waist, pulling me closer, and the intensity of the moment threatens to drown me. But as his kiss deepens, a cold wave of reality crashes over me.

This can't happen.

I push against his chest, breaking the kiss, my breathing ragged as I take a step back. "You're stupid to have done that," I whisper, my voice shaking. I want to stay in his arms, to let myself believe that this could work, but I can't. I step further away, clutching my towel tightly, my mind spinning. "I can't do this, Zayne. We can't."

Chapter 19

Zayne

Once again, I find myself back in my room, the silence pressing down on me like a weight. My thoughts drift to Kendall, as they always do, and before I can stop myself, my hand is on my cock, pumping with frustration. She's all I can think about—her stubbornness, the way she looks at me like she wants me but keeps pulling away. It's fucking tearing me apart. I bite down on my lip, trying to focus, but it's her that I want. Her face, her body, her soul—everything. Yet she refuses to give in to the emotions that wrap around us every time we're close.

"Fuck," I breathe out, my muscles tensing as I come, the anger bubbling up alongside the release. It's not enough. It's never enough. My hand isn't her, and I'm left feeling just as hollow as before. I stare down at the mess in my palm, disgusted with myself. I'm pissed—pissed at her for not wanting to stay, pissed at myself for not being able to make her see what we could have. Kendall admitted she's falling for me, so why the hell is she still talking about leaving?

I wipe my hand clean in the bathroom, splashing cold water on my face. She's tangled up in the damage her father's done to her over the years. I get it—hell, I *understand* it—but how can she not see that I'm different? I'd never hurt her the way her father or his men have. I would never raise a hand against her. I would never let anyone else touch her. She'd be my everything. *She is* my everything. And yet, it's not enough for her to stay.

Leaning against the sink, I stare at my reflection, the dark bags under my eyes a testament to how little sleep I've had since this all started. My mind spins with the plan—our plan—but I can't shake the feeling that if she leaves before we finish, I might never find her again. I have her alias, sure, but she's resourceful. If she wanted to disappear, she could. She'd become nothing more than a ghost haunting my past, and I can't fucking have that.

I've never been in love before. Never thought it was even possible for someone like me. But now, I'm knee-deep in this shit, chasing the daughter of my biggest rival like some lovesick idiot. I was supposed to be taking down Lyle, not falling for his goddamn daughter.

With a sigh, I leave the bathroom and head down to the lobby, the dim lights casting long shadows on the walls. I make myself a pot of coffee, the bitter scent filling the room, and sit down to work out the next part of our plan. We've got a few more men to take out—quickly, in the middle of the night, during a shootout. Clean and simple. But Lyle? He's a different story. He needs to be the last to go. He has to feel the full weight of everything he's built crumbling around him. I want him to experience the dread, the helplessness, the agony of losing everything before I finish him off.

But his death? His death will be special. It won't be quick like Dalton's. No, Lyle's screams will echo for hours, maybe even days. He'll beg for mercy, but none will come. His end will be drawn out, painful—exactly what Kendall deserves after what he's put her through. What Millie deserves after they tortured her out on the street.

Dalton wasn't supposed to die so soon. I'd planned to take my time with him, to make his last moments as agonizing as possible, but the bastard forced my hand. When he cornered Kendall in her house, I had no choice. He would have killed her, and I couldn't let that happen. Not her. Not Kendall.

Lyle won't get off that easy. His death will be slow, brutal. It'll be the kind of death that leaves a mark on the world, a scar that never heals. And Kendall? She'll have her revenge. She'll watch him fall, and maybe then—*maybe*—she'll see that I'm the only one who's ever truly been on her side. The only one who would tear the world apart for her.

The pull between us feels like a heavy fog, thickening the air as Kendall steps out from the dark hall. Her movements are slow, hesitant, like she's testing the waters. "May I?" she asks, her voice quiet but clear.

I nod, my eyes locking on her. "This is your place. You don't have to ask."

Even in the dim light, I can see her blush. It's subtle, but it's there—a vulnerability she rarely shows. "You looked deep in thought, and I didn't want to interrupt you," she says, her gaze flicking from the table to me.

"I was." My voice is low, contemplative. "Do you want to be a part of the last steps in this?"

Her eyes narrow slightly with curiosity, but there's a flicker of hesitation too. "What are they?"

"A shootout at the club. Your father will be taken... and tortured. So he feels what Millie felt before her death. So he feels what *you* have felt for years."

Her eyes meet mine, and I can see the sadness there—an ocean of pain that she's been holding onto for so long. It's buried deep, but it's there, lingering, waiting to spill over. I wonder if she knows just how strong she is for surviving all of this hell. To be able to sit here, knowing what's coming, and help bring down the very men who've caused her so much harm... it's more than most people could handle.

"How would I help?" she asks, her voice soft but steady.

"You won't go to the shootout." My tone hardens protectively. "I already let you walk back into that club once, not knowing if they'd believe you. I won't put you in harm's way again. But your father... you can help draw his death out. Make him pay for everything he's done to you. You deserve that closure, Kendall."

Her lips part, and for a moment, she looks unsure, lost in her own thoughts. "I'm not capable of that," she whispers. "I've never—"

"I'll be there." I cut her off gently, needing her to feel the sincerity behind my words. "I'll help you through it. You're strong, Kendall. So much stronger than you give yourself credit for."

She shakes her head, her voice barely above a whisper. "I'm not. I just pretend to be."

Her words slice through me, because I know she believes them. But she's wrong. She's so wrong. I stand, the chair scraping against the floor as I round the table. I spin her chair, placing myself between her legs, leaning in close enough that I can feel the warmth of her breath against my skin.

"Bullshit," I murmur, my voice deep, full of conviction. "I've seen you. Kendall Elliot, you have a strength most people wish for. You've survived more than anyone should ever have to. You're here, you're fighting back. That's real strength."

I can't stop myself—I lean in, pressing my lips to hers, soft at first, tentative, but full of meaning. It's a kiss filled with everything I haven't said, everything I've been holding back. Her lips respond slowly at first, then her hands trail up my chest, wrapping around my neck as if she's pulling me closer, needing the connection as much as I do.

The kiss deepens, growing more intense, more desperate. The walls we've both built around ourselves start to crumble as I lift her from the chair, carrying her to my room. Her body feels perfect in my arms, and when I lay her down on my bed, it's like she belongs there.

My hands roam her body, touching every inch of her, memorizing the way she feels beneath me. When my fingers trace the wet patch between her thighs, a soft moan escapes her lips, and it drives me wild. She's fighting it—fighting us—but I need her to stop. I need her to want this as badly as I do.

I lean in for another kiss, but she presses her hand gently against my chest, stopping me. Her eyes search mine, her voice barely above a whisper. "We can't go back from this," she says, the weight of her words hanging between us.

A slow grin spreads across my face, because I know what she's really asking. "I have no plans to."

For me, there's no going back. I'm all in—we are all in.

As I unbuckle her jeans, the sound of the zipper cuts through the quiet space between us. The soft material slides down her thighs, revealing smooth, bare skin. My fingers glide over her legs, feeling the goosebumps rising under my touch. I've seen her legs before, in shorts, bikinis, and a thong. But like this—bare, vulnerable, and fully exposed to me—it feels different. More intimate. The sight of her has me in awe.

I sit her up, my hands trailing along her back as I lift her shirt. My pulse quickens, every second feels like it's charged with electricity. Just as I'm about to pull the fabric over her head, my door bursts open with a loud thud.

"Shit," I mutter under my breath.

Killian stands there, one hand covering his eyes, the other waving blindly in the air. "We've got movement in the club," he says quickly before slamming the door shut behind him.

The moment shatters, and I look down at Kendall. The frustration claws at me, the urge to cry out from being deprived of her so suddenly. The connection we were building, the vulnerability we shared, it feels incomplete—left hanging in the air. I bite back my frustration, knowing there's no time to dwell on it. We have a job to do, and it's a dangerous one. The club is stirring, and there's no room for distractions.

I help her back into her clothes, my fingers trembling slightly as I pull her jeans up, as if I'm afraid this moment will slip away from us forever. Once she's dressed, I press a lingering kiss to her forehead, a silent promise that this isn't over.

Together, we head to the lobby where Killian and the rest of the crew are gathered, rubbing their eyes and waking from sleep as they crowd around the TV. The room is thick with anticipation, a different kind of tension now as we watch the live feed of disorder unfolding at Lyle's club.

Killian glances over at me, guilt flickering in his eyes. "Sorry about the timing," he says, nodding toward Kendall before pointing at the screen. "But you're gonna want to see this."

On the screen, cops swarm the club, their flashing lights illuminating the night as they pour through the doors. Lyle's voice is barely audible over the commotion, but we can make out his furious screams. He's pointing wildly at the officers, yelling accusations that make us all smirk.

"It was her!" Lyle's voice cracks as he thrashes against the officers. "My daughter's working with them! She's behind this! She's framing us! We're innocent!"

I glance at Kendall, her face pale as she watches her father unravel. The stern expression is a sharp contrast to the power she had just hours ago, manipulating the situation to perfection. Now, Lyle's losing control, and she knows it.

"My ass they're innocent," I mutter, crossing my arms as I lean back.

The camera zooms in on Lyle's office, where the cops sift through stacks of papers. And then, just as planned, they find it—the insurance claim, filed suspiciously a day before the bikes were torched. One of the officers holds it up, and the room goes still.

"How?" Kendall whispers, turning to me, her brows furrowed in confusion.

I nod toward Deylan, who stands off to the side with a satisfied smirk on his face. "Got our ways, beautiful," I tell her, giving her a small grin.

The truth is, Deylan had been the key to this part of the operation. While Kendall had distracted her father with the chaos surrounding Satchel and Dalton's betrayals, Deylan had slipped in undetected. Like a ghost, he moved through the shadows, planting the forged insurance papers just beneath the stack on Lyle's desk. It was flawless.

"That's not mine! I didn't file until after the explosion!" Lyle's voice rings out in desperation as they slap the cuffs on him.

I watch with satisfaction as Lyle is hauled off in handcuffs, his face flushed with rage and disbelief. His men will bail him out eventually, of course, but the damage is done. The corrupt cop they work with will help bury this but some of his men will question him now, doubting his loyalty. They'll wonder if he really destroyed their prized bikes just for a quick payout. And with the modifications Deylan made to the system, the insurance payout won't be nearly enough to cover the loss.

"Less than what it should've been, huh?" Kendall asks quietly, piecing it together.

I nod. "Much less. That's gonna sting when they find out."

Her lips twitch in a small, satisfied smile as she turns back to the screen. The plan is falling into place perfectly. Lyle is crumbling, his empire slowly slipping through his fingers, and with it, the hold he's had on her. This is only the beginning of his downfall, and soon, Kendall will finally have the revenge she deserves.

Chapter 20

Zayne

The rumble of our bikes reverberates through my chest, a low, steady vibration that grows more intense with every mile closer to the club. Lyle's club. After three days of radio silence, he was finally spotted there this morning, skulking back in after his release. The air is thick with anticipation, the tension evident as we ride in formation, the roar of engines drowning out any lingering doubt. Kendall hasn't answered a single one of his calls. He knows now—he has to. We've been playing him against his own people, and his empire is crumbling.

"If you see any of Knights, Dalton, or Kendall, you come to me first," Lyle had growled during his last meeting, his voice laced with paranoia and anger. "I want to end their fucking lives with my own two hands."

He's scared, and it's almost laughable how easy it's been to toy with him. He never once suspected that his cameras had been tampered with, that we were watching his every move. Hell, we've practically written it out for him—planting evidence of their past sins, exposing their attacks on women, and even having Kendall feed him bits of information when she went back to the club. We've played him like a fiddle, and he still doesn't see it.

But stupidity can still be dangerous. The Iron Guards have a reputation for a reason, and I'm genuinely surprised no other group has managed to take them down. Their arrogance makes them sloppy, but they're unpredictable, and that makes them deadly.

We pull up just past the parking lot, our bikes rolling to a halt behind a line of cars. The Sapphire looms ahead, silent but tense, like a beast ready to lash out. My heart pounds as I dismount, and my men follow suit, moving with quiet precision. Kendall wanted to come—she begged me to let her—but there was no way I'd let her near this place right now. Not when the real battle is about to begin.

Using the cars as cover, we line up, weapons at the ready. I take a deep breath, my finger resting lightly on the trigger. Then, in unison, we each fire one shot, the bullets slamming into the brick facade of the building in a perfect line.

The ricochet echoes, and a moment later, Lyle charges outside, his face a twisted mask of fury. He stares at the bullet holes, eyes wide as the reality of the situation sinks in. He knows he's outmatched. With a panicked glance, he rushes back inside.

Killian crouches beside me, his phone in hand, the live feed from inside the club displayed on the screen. "He's gathering everyone in the storage room," he whispers. "All the customers are being shoved into the back for protection."

Good. No innocents.

With a nod, I signal the men, and we let loose. Gunfire erupts, tearing through the quiet night. The bullets shred through the walls, ripping apart the siding, blowing chunks of brick, and sending glass raining down in a glittering cascade. The sound is deafening—gunshots, shattering windows, the screams of men inside scrambling for cover.

Then Lyle's men pour out, weapons in hand, firing back. They're not trained like us, not tactical. They're wild, shooting without precision, and it's clear they're acting out of desperation.

"Remember!" I shout over the noise, my voice commanding and clear. "Lyle lives. Kill the rest. No innocent deaths."

My men move with practiced efficiency, picking off Lyle's crew one by one. It's brutal and fast, the firefight exploding in a storm of bullets and blood. Bodies fall, and the club, once a fortress of power, is quickly reduced to a battleground.

Lyle's nowhere in sight, still hiding like the coward he is. But he'll come out eventually. He has no choice. His empire is crumbling around him, and all that's left is for him to watch it fall.

A bullet whizzes past my ear, barely missing me, and I duck behind a car. The return fire is fierce, but my men stay focused, trained for this exact moment. I glance at Killian, who's still tracking everything on his phone.

"They're thinning out," he says. "Won't be long now."

I grit my teeth, eyes scanning the building, waiting for that one final moment—when Lyle steps into the light, realizing his reign of terror is over.

One by one, Lyle's men keep falling, their bodies hitting the ground and the rest panicking as they scramble to retreat back inside the club. The retreat gives us the perfect opening. Silently, we circle around the building, moving like shadows through the dark alleyway and slipping into the dressing room through the back. The muffled sounds of retreating footsteps echoing through the hallway.

I motion for my men to stay close, and we creep forward, closing in on Lyle and the last of his crew. They're in the lobby, huddled together, frantic whispers filling the air as they try to figure out their next move. But they don't know we're already here.

The moment we're in position, the silence shatters. Gunfire erupts once more, the room exploding in chaos. His remaining men go down fast, their bodies crumpling to the floor, leaving only Lyle, the so-called king of this crumbling empire, alive. He's not standing tall like the ruthless leader he pretends to be. Instead, he's cowering like a rat beneath one of the tables, his hands shaking as he pleads for his life.

"Please—please, don't kill me!" he stammers, his voice cracking with desperation. "Please have mercy."

I step forward, the cold weight of my gun steady in my hand as my men fan out behind me, keeping their aim locked in case Lyle decides to try something stupid. "Mercy?" I repeat, my voice laced with a bitter laugh. "Where was the mercy for Millie, Lyle? Or any of the other women you and your men destroyed?"

His eyes dart around the room, his face pale as he stammers, "I—I don't know what you're talking about."

My blood boils at his pathetic attempt to lie. "No? Let me refresh your memory."

With a flick of my hand, the screens around the club burst to life. Every monitor, every projector, fills with the haunting footage of Millie—tied up, beaten, and brutalized by Lyle's men. Her screams pierce the heavy air, echoing off the walls like ghosts from the past. It's impossible to ignore, impossible for Lyle to hide from now.

The people in the back—the innocents we've kept safe—begin to pour out of the storage room. Their faces pale as they hear the gut-wrenching sounds of Millie's torment. Some cry out, others cover their mouths in shock. They rush out into the lobby, their eyes wide with horror as they see the bodies of Lyle's men strewn across the floor, lifeless.

When they spot me, still standing tall among the carnage, I nod toward the front door. "You're free to go," I say, my voice calm and cold as they scramble to leave. They don't need to witness what comes next.

This moment, the one I've been waiting for, belongs to me and Lyle.

His eyes are locked on the screens, his body trembling. He tries to crawl backward, desperate to distance himself from the truth, but there's nowhere left to run. Nowhere left to hide.

I step closer, my boots crunching over broken glass, debris, and his dead men as I close the distance between us. He flinches, his mouth opening and closing like a fish gasping for air.

"Please—please," he sobs, his eyes wild with fear. "I'll give you anything. Money, power—whatever you want, it's yours."

"What I want," I growl, crouching down so I'm eye level with him, "is for you to feel what you made her feel. I want you to experience every ounce of fear, every scream, every last moment of suffering."

His face crumples, and tears spill down his cheeks, but I don't feel an ounce of sympathy. He brought this on himself.

"Millie was innocent," I continue, my voice low and deadly. "She didn't deserve what you did to her. None of the women you've hurt did. And now, it's your turn to suffer."

I grab him by the collar, yanking him out from under the table, and drag him toward the center of the room. The footage of Millie still plays on the screens, a haunting backdrop to the moment we've all waited for. Lyle tries to beg, tries to plead, but his words fall on deaf ears.

This isn't a negotiation. This is justice.

Chapter 21

Kendall

The pacing in the lobby feels endless, the silence only amplifying the knot of fear tightening in my stomach. I've been counting the minutes—each one passing feels like a hammer driving nails into my nerves. Zayne's been gone over two hours now, and the anxiety has wrapped itself around me like a noose. What if something went wrong? What if they're all dead? My mind keeps conjuring images of Zayne, lying on the cold ground somewhere, lifeless. I try to push the thoughts away, but they claw back, more vivid each time.

He took my Mustang keys, making it clear that I was meant to stay out of the fight. But the thought of sitting here, helpless, while my father might still be out there, free and dangerous, is too much to bear. If Zayne doesn't come back, I'm next. I know it. My father will stop at nothing to make me pay for betraying him, and without Zayne, I'll have no one left to protect me.

I throw on my Chuck Taylors, my leather jacket, and grab the bag with my new identity. If Zayne doesn't return, I'll walk to the club, see for myself what's left of the battlefield. At least then I'll know the truth, even if it means fleeing on foot to escape whatever's coming. As I push open the lobby door, the low rumble of engines in the distance makes my heart leap into my throat.

The bikes come into view, their headlights piercing through the night, and I spot him—Zayne—leading his men back to the hotel. Relief crashes into me, so overwhelming it steals my breath for a moment. I drop my bag and sprint outside, my legs moving faster than I thought possible. The second he throws his leg over his bike, I leap into his arms, holding him as if letting go would mean losing him for real.

His strong arms wrap around me, and he pulls back, his eyes searching mine. "Hey, you okay?" he asks, concern etched into every line of his face.

Tears spill over my cheeks, my voice barely a whisper. "You took so long... I thought you'd gotten yourself killed."

He brushes a thumb across my cheek, wiping away the tears, his own expression softening. "We're okay. No casualties on our part."

Relief floods me, but then reality crashes back in. "What about my father and his men?"

Zayne's gaze hardens. "His men are all dead. Your father is being transported here." His voice is steady, but I can tell he's holding something back.

As if on cue, a truck pulls up, and Killian drags my father out from the back. His head is covered by a black bag, his hands bound. Zayne presses a finger to his lips, a smile tugging at the corner of his mouth. "Stay quiet," he whispers. "I want him to see you later. The look on his face will be priceless."

Inside, they secure my father in one of the spare rooms upstairs, making sure the cameras are on him at all times. There's no chance he's getting free, not without us knowing. Once he's out of sight, the atmosphere shifts.

The tension that's clung to Zayne's men since this all started finally seems to dissipate. They gather around, cracking open beers, laughing, sharing stories about the shootout like it's just another day in their world. They're relaxed, at ease in a way I've never seen before. But I can't share their relief. Not when the weight of what comes next presses down on me like a tidal wave.

This is almost over. The revenge, the abuse, the violence—it's nearly done. But what comes after? As I watch Zayne from across the room, my chest tightens. He's smiling, clinking bottles with his men, but all I can think about is the moment I'll have to say goodbye.

I slip away from the group, unnoticed, and head to my room. The bag with my new identity sits on the bed, staring back at me, a reminder of the path I've chosen. I sink down onto the mattress, the tears falling freely now. I bury my face in the pillow and cry, not just for the life I've escaped, but for the love I'm walking away from.

I want Zayne. God, do I want him. I want the future he's promised, the love he's shown me, the safety I feel in his arms. But I know what staying with him means—staying in this life, the one I've fought so hard to escape. Being with him means trading one cage for another, even if his is gilded with love.

Zayne can't walk away from this life. He's built into it, molded by it. And as much as I wish I could stay, I know I can't. I want freedom, and with Zayne, that's something I'll never truly have.

I'll have to walk away from him, even if it breaks my heart to do it. Because loving him means staying trapped in a world I can't survive in. But I don't know if I can survive without him either.

The knock on my door is soft, almost hesitant, but it echoes through the heavy silence of the room. I'm still lying on the bed, curled up in the mess of my tangled sheets, tears hot on my face. When I open the door, I'm met by Peyton. His eyes are solemn, his expression grateful, but I can't find the strength to smile.

"Thank you," he says, his voice quiet but firm. "For helping us get justice for Millie."

I nod, the lump in my throat making it impossible to respond. My chest tightens, my breath comes in shallow bursts. Peyton stands there for a moment longer, his eyes searching mine as if he wants to say more. But he doesn't. He turns and walks away, leaving me alone again with the knowledge that this is the beginning of the end. The final steps of this twisted journey.

I close the door softly, the latch clicking into place sounding like a prison door locking me in. I crawl back into bed, the weight of everything pulling me deeper into the mattress. Tomorrow, the last part of the revenge will take place. Once my father's life is gone, once the final thread tying me to this nightmare is cut, I'll have nothing left here.

In the stillness of the night, I drift off, but I'm startled awake by the shifting of the mattress beneath me. I blink in the darkness, my heart skipping a beat until I recognize the familiar figure lying beside me. Zayne.

His breath is heavy with the scent of alcohol, and his eyes are glazed, lost in the haze of drunkenness. He opens his arms without a word, and I fall into them, pressing my face against the warmth of his chest. His heart beats against my cheek, a steady rhythm that lulls me back into a fragile sense of comfort. I breathe him in, letting his scent wrap around me, grounding me in a moment I know can't last.

Morning comes too soon. The soft light seeps through the curtains, casting a pale glow across the room. I feel him stir, his arm slowly slipping from beneath me. I blink, still groggy, and watch as he sits at the edge of the bed, pulling on his boots. The sound of the laces sliding through the eyelets fills the air, each tug reminding me of the inevitable.

Without thinking, I move toward him, wrapping my arms and legs around his waist, pressing my face into the solid warmth of his back. I can feel the tightness in his muscles, the way his breath catches as my touch lingers. His heart pounds beneath my cheek, picking up speed like it's racing against time.

He turns, his face inches from mine, and there's that smile—small, tender, like he's trying to hold onto something that's already slipping through his fingers. "Morning," he whispers.

"Morning," I reply, my voice barely audible.

His eyes search mine, and I can see the question there before he even speaks. "You ready?"

I shake my head, the words spilling from me without hesitation. "No."

He leans in, his lips brushing mine in a soft, lingering kiss. It feels like a goodbye, like he's trying to imprint himself on me in this fleeting moment, hoping that somehow it will change what we both know is coming. His hands find my hips, pulling me closer as he pushes me back onto the bed, settling between my thighs, his mouth never leaving mine.

The kiss deepens, desperate and raw, like he's trying to convince me—convince himself—that we can hold on a little longer. When he pulls back, his breath is ragged, his forehead resting against mine. "I'm not ready to lose you," he murmurs, his voice thick with emotion.

I close my eyes, the truth tearing at my chest. "I was never yours to lose," I whisper, my words cruel but necessary.

He pulls back just enough to look at me, his eyes full of pain. "I want you to be. So badly." I reach up, cupping his face in my hands, memorizing the feel of his skin under my fingers. His warmth, his strength, everything I've come to love. "What can I do to make you stay?" His voice cracks, and the vulnerability in it makes my heart ache.

I shake my head slowly. "You can't do what I'd ask of you, Zayne. It wouldn't be fair."

His jaw tightens, his grip on me firming as if he could keep me here by sheer will. "Name it," he pleads. "I'll make it happen."

Tears prick my eyes as I whisper, "You can't walk away from your men. You can't leave this life behind."

"Damn it, Kendall," he growls, his voice breaking. "You're going to kill me when you leave. Why did I have to fall in love with you?"

I pull him close, kissing him again, feeling the weight of every word he's saying. "I've asked myself the same about you," I say softly, my lips brushing his.

He presses his forehead to mine, his breath shaky. "I love you," he says, his voice barely audible, but the emotion in it is deafening.

Through the tears, I force the words out. "I love you too, Zayne." And with that, I pull away, slipping out of bed and into my shoes. The room feels colder, emptier now. We both know this is it.

I follow him into the lobby, where the strong scent of coffee hangs in the air, heavy and familiar. This is it—the last morning we'll have together before I have to face my father, before I have to face the truth.

And soon, I'll have to face leaving Zayne behind, too.

Chapter 22

Zayne

Our footsteps thud dully against the carpet, the weight of what's about to happen pressing down with each step as we approach the room where Lyle is tied up. The air in the hallway is thick with anticipation, and my stomach churns with a mix of adrenaline and disgust. At the door, I place a hand on Kendall's arm, signaling for her to stay back for a moment. She nods, her face set in cold determination, but I can see the undercurrent of emotion running beneath the surface.

The door creaks as I push it open, and inside, the stench of sweat, piss, and fear hits me like a wave. Lyle is slumped on the floor, his back against the bedpost, his wrists tied harshly behind him. A wet stain spreads beneath him, and the sight of it confirms what I already knew—he's been reduced to a sniveling coward. The man who once ruled with cruelty and terror is now nothing more than a shell of himself.

Killian and I walk in, our boots thudding against the hard floor. I stop directly in front of him, staring down at the man who's caused so much pain. His lips tremble, eyes wild with fear, and when he speaks, his voice is hoarse, barely a whisper.

"P-Please," he stammers, his breath coming in shaky gasps.

I crouch down, meeting his eyes with a smirk curling on my lips. "P-P-Please," I mock, my voice dripping with disdain as I get right in his face. I can smell the fear on him—like a man who knows death is standing just inches away.

He flinches, his gaze darting nervously around the room before landing on me again. "Where's Kendall?" he asks, his voice rising with desperation.

I lean back, crossing my arms over my chest. "Oh, *now* you're worried about her? Or do you just want to see her one last time before you die?"

"I—I want to apologize to her," he mumbles, the words sounding weak even to his own ears.

Killian lets out a deep, dark laugh and kneels beside me. "Apologize? Why now? Because you're tied up, pissing yourself like the worthless piece of shit you are? You think that makes up for years of what you did to her?"

Lyle's tears stream down his face, his sobs pitiful and soft. The sight of him, broken and begging, makes me reel with anger. He's fucking pathetic. I stand, my body tense with disgust, and move toward the door. With a nod, I signal to Kendall that it's time.

She walks in, her steps steady and deliberate. The moment she steps through the doorway, the energy in the room shifts. There's a storm in her eyes, a quiet fury that burns behind the calm exterior. She stops a few feet away from him, looking down at the man who tried to break her.

"Hi, *Dad*," she sneers, her voice laced with venom. "Guess you're not so tough without your men here to protect you, huh?"

Lyle's head snaps up at the sound of her voice, and his eyes widen. "Kendall, darling. Please." His voice cracks, and it's almost comical watching him scramble for any shred of control. "If you help me, I swear I'll never hurt you again."

Kendall steps forward, her eyes never leaving his. "No," she says, her voice steady. "You'll just have your men do it, right? You'll find another way to make my life hell."

Lyle shakes his head frantically, the panic rising in him. "Never again," he pleads, his tears falling freely now. "I swear."

Kendall's lips twist into a bitter smile. "You know, for years I wondered if you'd ever say those words. If you'd ever actually feel sorry for anything you did." She takes another step closer, her body rigid with the weight of everything she's endured. "But now, standing here, seeing you like this? I realize something. I don't need your apology."

She looks at him like he's nothing. Like he's already dead.

"Well, it was nice talking to you," she says coldly. "But I have other things to do."

Killian stands and grabs Lyle by the collar, yanking him to his feet with one swift motion. His arms are stretched painfully behind him, bound tightly at the wrists, and he lets out a sharp cry of pain. I step beside Kendall, my hand on the small of her back as we watch. Lyle's breath comes in panicked gasps, his eyes darting between us as if searching for some shred of mercy.

But there is none.

This is the end. He's finally going to feel the fear, the helplessness, the pain that he's inflicted on others for so long. And as he stands there, trembling, tears and snot dripping down his face, I know that no matter what happens next, Kendall is free.

Lyle's pitiful scream echoes through the room, but none of us react. His voice, once so full of arrogance and cruelty, now wavers like a cornered animal. I step forward, my hand sliding to the sheath at my side, and pull out my knife. The black handle gleams under the dim light, the red knight engraved on it catching his wide, terrified eyes.

"You see this?" I ask, holding the knife up for him to see, letting him focus on it. His breath hitches, and I flick the blade open with a soft *click*. The sharp edge catches the light, and Lyle's scream rips through the silence. His body trembles so hard, the ropes binding him to the bedpost strain with the weight of his panic.

"I plunged this knife into Dalton's stomach and chest when he tried to kill Kendall in her house." My voice is cold, matter-of-fact, as if discussing the weather.

"He'd never!" Lyle bellows, shaking his head in denial, his voice cracking.

"Oh yeah?" I tilt my head, my lips curling into a cruel smile. I pull out my phone, tapping the screen until the feed from Kendall's house plays. I make sure he sees it clearly—the moment Dalton kicks Kendall in the stomach, her body crumpling, gasping for air. And then, with sickening precision, Dalton presses his boot down on her chest, grinding his heel into her throat, cutting off her breath.

Lyle's face drains of color as he watches, his mouth hanging open in disbelief. "No. He loved her. He'd never." His words are desperate now, clinging to a false reality, the one where he still holds power. His eyes flicker, darting between the three of us like a cornered animal searching for escape.

Kendall's voice cuts through the air, sharp and unyielding. "He'd done it to others. What stopped him from doing it to me?" Her composure is flawless, but I can feel the weight of her pain simmering beneath the surface. She's controlling it, refusing to let her father see the tears she might once have shed for him.

"He loved you," Lyle insists again, shaking his head as if repeating the lie could somehow make it true.

"No," Kendall says, her voice cold and final. "He loved control."

Her words hang in the air like a sentence. Lyle flinches, as if struck by the weight of them. I raise the knife, and before I even move, Lyle's body convulses in terror, his pleading filling the room like a broken record.

"Please! No! I'm sorry! I'll do anything!"

The first cut doesn't belong to me. I let the moment stretch, and with a sharp whistle, I signal

Peyton. The door creaks open, and Peyton steps in, his shadow long against the wall as he stalks toward Lyle like a predator closing in on its prey. Lyle's eyes widen with realization, recognition blooming in his gaze.

"You recognize me, don't you?" Peyton's voice is low, controlled, but every word drips with the fury of a man long consumed by vengeance. He reaches out, and I hand him the knife, its weight shifting into his grip like it was always meant for him.

"You're the girl's husband," Lyle whispers, his voice trembling, his eyes darting to the floor as if he can hide from Peyton's burning gaze.

"Woman," Peyton corrects, his voice dangerously calm. "She was a woman, and a wonderful one at that. And you took her from me." The pain in his voice is raw, but it only fuels his fury. In one swift motion, Peyton raises the knife and slashes at Lyle's arm. Blood seeps from the wound, dark and thick, dripping down Lyle's hand and pooling on the floor beneath him.

"I'm sorry! I'm sorry!" Lyle sobs, his entire body shaking.

"No, you're not," Peyton says, his voice icy and cutting. "You're only sorry we came for revenge. You didn't even know I was part of the Crimson Knights, did you? If you had, you'd have killed me long before it came to this."

Peyton steps forward again, his eyes locked on Lyle's trembling form. With cold precision, he slices across Lyle's other arm, the blade carving deep, parallel lines. Blood drips freely now, staining the floor in slow, rhythmic splatters.

"You killed the love of my life for *what*?" Peyton snarls, the fury in his voice reaching a crescendo. He grabs the front of Lyle's shirt, slicing through the fabric with ease, baring his chest to us. The cuts are shallow but deliberate, marking him like the shame he's earned. Each slash is a reflection of the lives he's destroyed, the pain he's caused, the evil he's allowed to flourish.

"Kendall, please!" Lyle cries out, his voice cracking, his eyes wild as they land on his daughter. He's no longer the monstrous figure he once was. Now, he's nothing but a weak, broken man, laid bare before the people who refuse to let him escape his sins.

Kendall stands there, watching him, her expression unreadable. But I can see it—she's done. The girl who once trembled before this man, who feared his power, is gone. In her place stands a woman who knows her strength, who has faced her demons and come out victorious.

She shakes her head, her gaze cold and unforgiving. "You're not even worth hating anymore," she says quietly, and her words land like a final blow. Lyle's sobs echo in the room, but they fall on deaf ears.

He's lost. Finally.

Chapter 23

Kendall

Peyton carves *Millie* into my father's chest, each letter shallow yet searing, a constant reminder of the woman he destroyed to take to the grave with him. The blood seeps slowly from the cuts, not deep enough to kill, but enough to make him scream in agony. I watch, unmoved. I've felt that pain before—Dalton used to do the same to me, leaving cuts when I would *misbehave*—but today, it's my father who's powerless and broken.

Once Peyton finishes his work, Killian ties my father's chest to the post so he can't sit and steps forward, taking his time as he etches a knight into my father's stomach. His hand is steady, his movements slow, like an artist perfecting a gruesome masterpiece on human flesh. My father's screams echo off the walls, sharp and desperate, but they don't reach outside the room. No one outside this place will hear his cries for mercy. The men downstairs are watching this play out on the TV, as if it's a show. For years, it was me screaming, pleading. But now, it's him.

And I smirk at the sound.

When Killian finishes, he hands the knife to Zayne. The cruel smile that spreads across Zayne's face chills the air. "This is for Millie," he says, driving the knife through my father's left hand with brutal precision. My father howls as Zayne rips the blade free, only to drive it into his left wrist. "This is for Annette," Zayne growls. Each stab, each name is another woman my father and his men tormented.

"This is for Emily," Zayne continues, the knife plunging into my father's arm again. The blood flows freely now, soaking his shirt, his skin becoming a canvas of every life he ruined. I remember when Zayne showed me the list of women, each name accompanied by undeniable proof of my father's hand in their suffering. I cried for hours that night. I knew he was evil, but seeing it all laid out like that—the sheer scale of his cruelty—made me realize he wasn't just a monster. He was the devil himself.

And then Zayne turns to me. His eyes are dark, and there's a weight to his words when he says, "and this, this is for Kendall." He flips the knife, offering the handle to me. I stare at it for a second, the blade gleaming with fresh blood, then slowly I reach out and take it.

The room feels like it's holding its breath.

I step forward, the weight of Zayne, Killian, and Peyton behind me, solid and unwavering. My father looks at me, his face contorted in pain, fear stark in his eyes. He's trembling, his voice gone. For the first time in my life, he's afraid of me.

I exhale a long, shaky breath. "Fuck you, Dad," I say, my voice raw with years of pain, rage, and betrayal.

The first stab lands in his shoulder. His scream rips through the room, piercing and broken, but I'm beyond hearing it now. I pull the knife free and stab him again, this time in the chest. I can feel the rush of emotions unraveling—years of pent-up anger and helplessness flooding out with every plunge of the blade.

I stab him over and over, my movements wild, uncontrollable. His arms, his chest, his neck, his face—there's nothing left untouched as I tear him apart, screaming through gritted teeth. With each stab, I think of every time he forced me to perform for his men as a child, every night I was forced on stage, every time he let Dalton beat me, every time he used me instead of protecting me.

He stole my childhood, broke me, twisted me into something that had to fight for survival. Now, it's him being shredded, turned into nothing more than a bloody pulp under the weight of my rage.

By the time Zayne steps forward, gently laying a hand over mine, I'm shaking uncontrollably. He pries the knife from my trembling fingers, but I barely notice. My body is numb, my mind racing, and my vision blurs with unshed tears.

I stumble back, my knees giving out beneath me, and Killian is there, catching me as I fall apart. The adrenaline, the rage—it all drains away, leaving only exhaustion and a hollow ache where my anger once burned so bright.

As Peyton spits on my father's body and leaves the room, Zayne pulls me into his arms. His hands stroke through my hair, his voice a soft murmur, shushing me, comforting me, holding me together when I feel like I might break.

In the distance, I hear Killian make the call. The cleaners will come soon, wiping away all traces of my father from this place, erasing him from the world as if he never existed. But I will always carry him, in the scars he left on my soul.

But today, for the first time, I'm free. I'm not afraid anymore. He can't hurt me ever again. And the weight of that, the enormity of my own survival, breaks me down into sobs as Zayne holds me tight.

After I calm down, I head to my room for a shower, to cleanse my father's blood off me. The hot water washes over me, but it does nothing to cleanse the weight pressing down on my chest. I scrub harder, my skin reddening under my hands, as if trying to erase the memories, the blood, the screams. But it's all still there, lingering in the steam and clinging to me like a second skin.

When I step out of the shower, the mirror is fogged, obscuring my reflection. Maybe it's better that way. I towel off quickly and dress in silence, pulling on a pair of jeans and a hoodie, something simple. My body moves on autopilot as I pack the few belongings I brought into my bag. The room is quiet, too quiet, save for the soft hum of the ceiling fan, and it feels suffocating. I know Zayne will come to check on me soon—he always does. He'll knock on the door, asking if I'm okay, offering to stay with me. His presence, as comforting as it is, won't change what I know I have to do.

I sling the bag over my shoulder, my heart racing as I glance around the room one last time. This isn't a goodbye I want to say in person. Not to him. Not to the man who saved me, who showed me what love could be. It would be too hard, and I've already made my choice.

Quietly, I slip out the back door, careful not to let it creak. The evening air is crisp, biting against my wet hair, and I shiver, though not entirely from the cold. My bright green Mustang is parked just a few steps away, gleaming under the post lights, my escape plan set in motion. The roar of the engine as I start it feels both exhilarating and gut-wrenching at the same time. This is it. There's no turning back.

I shift into gear, the tires crunching over gravel as I pull away from the old hotel. The road stretches out before me like an invitation to freedom, but my chest tightens with every mile I put between me and them. Between me and Zayne.

My hands grip the steering wheel tighter as I hit the interstate. I floor it, the engine growling beneath me as the Mustang surges forward, speed blurring the lights on the side of the highway. I don't look back. I can't. If I let myself even glance in the rearview mirror, I might lose the strength to keep going. And I can't afford to second-guess myself now. Not after everything.

The memories of the past few hours swirl in my mind like a storm, chaotic and consuming. My father's lifeless body, the way Zayne held me as I broke apart, the twisted satisfaction I felt as I finally took control of my life. And yet, that control also means walking away from the only person who's ever truly understood me.

Zayne, the man I love, the man who would give up anything for me—anything except his club. His loyalty to his brothers is something I can't ask him to abandon, and staying with him would mean staying in that life. A life I've fought so hard to escape.

Tears blur my vision, but I don't slow down. The highway stretches endlessly before me, the open road beckoning me to the unknown. Saugatuck, Michigan. It's a place I chose at random, a small town near Lake Michigan, where I can disappear. A fresh start, far from the blood and violence that have shadowed my every step. A new life.

I'll drive through the night, the weight of my decision settling deeper with every passing mile. The hum of the engine becomes a comforting drone, a rhythm that matches the beat of my heart, steady but heavy. My thoughts drift to Zayne, to the way he smiled at me this morning, to the way he kissed me like he was trying to memorize the feel of my lips. He didn't know that was our last kiss. He didn't know that I'm truly leaving him behind, along with the wreckage of my old life.

But he'll figure it out soon enough. If he hasn't already gone to my room to console me.

The sky begins to lighten as dawn approaches, the dark horizon softening into shades of blue and pink. I wipe at my tear-streaked face, my heart aching as I realize I'm really doing this. I really left him.

I take a deep breath, my foot steady on the gas. The road ahead is long, but for the first time in my life, it's mine to choose. No more fear. No more control. Just me, the open road, and whatever lies ahead in the quiet solitude of a Michigan town that has no idea who I am or where I came from.

But as the sun breaks over the horizon, painting the sky with gold with a brand new day, I whisper softly, "Goodbye, Zayne."

Chapter 24

Kendall

The bell above the door dings, echoing softly in the quiet library as I shuffle through the stack of returned books from yesterday. I don't look up, offering my usual greeting to whoever has just walked in, my hands busy organizing the novels into their proper places. The weight of the books, the soft rustle of paper, and the scent of old books bring a sense of calm that I've come to love about my new life in Saugatuck. It's been serene, tranquil—exactly what I needed.

Life here has been a balm to the wounds I didn't know how to heal. The days are slow, peaceful. I spend my mornings at the lake, my afternoons at the library, and my evenings curled up with a good book in my small, cozy apartment just outside of town. It's a far cry from the hell I left behind, but it's mine. I smile to myself, placing the last of the returned books on the shelf. Raiven is the only connection I've kept from my past. She's sworn never to tell anyone she's in contact with me, especially Zayne. I didn't reach out until I was sure he had gone back to Atlanta, resuming his life, leaving me behind as just a memory.

But I've kept tabs on him. Zayne is still out there, avenging the innocent, bringing justice to women like me. Sometimes, late at night, I wonder if he's met someone new, someone who can share his life without the weight of the past pulling them down. But then I shake the thought away, reminding myself that I made the right choice by leaving. Even now, there's a dull ache in my chest, a small hollow space where he once was.

Still, I'm free. Truly free. I make my own decisions now, without fear or anyone controlling me. My father's disappearance had been labeled as him fleeing from the law, a convenient story after the insurance fraud scheme he had been involved in went public. There were whispers that he had turned on his own men, killed them, and vanished into the wind. The case had gone cold, and with it, the last ties to the life I left behind.

None of the customers from that night dared to speak up against Zayne and his men. They'd witnessed firsthand the kind of terror my father could unleash, a visceral reminder of what happens to those who cross him. Fear is a powerful silencer, and the memory of that brutality ensured their loyalty wasn't given—it was forced. Each of them had made the same choice: to look the other way and keep their mouths shut, self-preservation outweighing the pull of justice.

The doorbell chimes again, and I call out another greeting without turning around. The small town has embraced me as "Rebecca", a quiet woman who loves books and keeps to herself. I've become part of the fabric here, unnoticed, unseen. It's exactly what I wanted.

I place the last book on the shelf, feeling the lightness of my workload for the day, when someone taps me gently on the shoulder. My body tenses instinctively, a ripple of unease washing over me. Slowly, I turn, and the breath leaves my lungs in a rush.

Zayne stands before me, his presence like a lightning strike in the middle of my quiet world. His dark hair is longer than when I last saw him, and his eyes, though still intense, hold a softness that wasn't there before. A faint smile plays at the corners of his lips as he looks at me, and I can see the mixture of emotions in his eyes—relief, affection, and something deeper, something I thought I'd never see again.

"Hey," he says, his voice low and familiar. It's the same voice that once whispered promises into the dark. "I'm looking for a woman. About five foot two, blonde hair, green eyes, drives a bright green Mustang. You wouldn't happen to have seen her around, would you?"

My heart pounds in my chest, and my voice barely works. "What are you doing here?" I manage to ask, my throat tight. It's been a year since I left him in that hotel, and I thought he would have moved on by now. I thought he would have let me go.

"Well," he says with a shrug, but his eyes never leave mine, "you see, I had Oliver working on finding you. And he finally got a hit."

I blink, my mind racing. Oliver. Of course, Zayne's trusted brother in the club. I should've known it wouldn't be that easy to disappear.

"Hey, Rebecca, you good?" My coworker, Harlow, calls out from behind a shelf, her voice casual but curious.

"Yes," I call back, trying to steady my shaking voice. "All good."

But it isn't. Not even close. Zayne's presence throws everything off balance. The peaceful life I've built here feels like it's on the verge of shattering, the cracks forming the moment I saw him standing in front of me.

I pull myself together, forcing a breath through my lungs. "You shouldn't have come," I say softly, though my heart aches at the sight of him. "I left for a reason, Zayne."

He tilts his head slightly, his eyes searching mine. "Yeah, and I let you go. For a while. But I couldn't forget about you, Kendall." The sound of my real name on his lips feels like both a blessing and a curse. "I couldn't stop thinking about you."

I look away, my hands gripping the edge of the cart. "I've moved on. I have a new life here. I'm happy."

Zayne steps closer, closing the distance between us. "Are you?" His voice is gentle but insistent. "Are you really happy, or are you just pretending to be?"

His words hit a nerve, and I feel the familiar sting of unshed tears. "I am happy," I whisper, more to convince myself than him.

He doesn't push me further. Instead, he just looks at me, that same calm, unwavering gaze that always made me feel like he could see straight through me. "I'm not here to drag you back,

Kendall. I'm here because I needed to see you. To make sure you're okay."

I swallow hard, my emotions swirling in a confusing mix of longing, guilt, and anger. "You shouldn't have come," I repeat, my voice barely audible.

"I know," he says, his voice softer now. "But I couldn't stay away."

For a moment, neither of us speaks, the silence thick between us. Finally, I take a deep breath and meet his gaze again. "What now?" I ask, the question hanging heavy in the air.

"I don't know," Zayne admits, his eyes softening as he looks at me. "But I had to see you."

I close my eyes for a moment, the weight of his words settling over me. What now, indeed?

"I get off at five. I'll meet you by my car." The words hang in the air as I turn back to my work, the dragging of time for that moment churning my insides. Each tick of the clock feels like a countdown to something monumental, and I'm acutely aware of how the thought of being alone with Zayne electrifies me. I shake with uncertainty, a nervous energy coursing through me at the prospect of being back in his arms again, knowing he wants me to come home with him.

When five finally arrives, I step outside, my heart racing. The evening sun bathes the parking lot in a golden hue, casting long shadows that flicker across the pavement. And there he is. Leaning casually against the driver's side of my Mustang, Zayne looks like he stepped out of my memories—solid, captivating, and impossibly real. My breath catches in my throat as I walk toward him, a whirlwind of emotions swirling within me.

As I approach, he stands straight, his posture exuding a mix of confidence and warmth. He opens his arms, and without hesitation, I rush into him, wrapping my arms around his strong frame. The moment feels electric, and I relish the familiar scent of him, the warmth of his body against mine. It's as if the world around us fades away, leaving just the two of us suspended in time.

"Did you ride your bike all the way here?" I ask, pulling back slightly to look into his eyes, searching for that glimmer of mischief I've always adored.

"No, I brought Killian's Camaro," he replies, his voice smooth and teasing.

"Where is it?" I inquire, a spark of curiosity igniting within me.

"He has it," Zayne replies, a playful smile dancing on his lips, his eyes glinting with that familiar mischief that always made my heart race.

I can't help but smile back, a rush of warmth flooding me at the sight of him. Then, in a moment that feels suspended in time, he leans down, capturing my lips with his. The kiss is soft at first, but it quickly deepens, igniting a familiar fire within me. Everything around us fades into oblivion—the library, the town, even the weight of the past—and for a brief moment, it's just us, lost in each other.

But the bliss is short-lived. The deep rumble of an engine pulls me back to reality, breaking the spell. I pull away, breathless, just as Killian parks beside my car and steps out. His black hair is streaked with a fiery red, a new look that somehow suits him. He walks toward us, a smile spreading across his face as he spots Zayne and me wrapped up in our embrace.

"Look at you two," he says, an amused glint in his eyes. He nods at me, and I return the gesture, my heart swelling at the sight of him. He's smiling instead of scowling.

"What now?" I ask Zayne.

"I was hoping you'd take me to see the place you call home. Maybe tomorrow we can sightsee some of your favorite spots," he replies, his eyes sparkling with excitement.

"Zayne—" I start, but he cuts me off.

"Don't push me away, Kendall. Give me this, please. Let me visit with you this one time. If by the time I leave, you still don't want to be with me, then I'll go and leave you alone."

Tears prick at my eyes. "It's not that I don't want you, Zayne."

"It's that you don't want to be controlled. You won't be. I promise a million times over, you'll have all the freedom you want. You'll just have me to love you as well." He leans in close to me, his voice dropping to a whisper. "Tomorrow morning. Meet me at the steakhouse downtown."

"Okay," I whisper, my heart pounding in my chest as I pull away and out of his arms.

As I drive away, I glance in the rearview mirror, watching them stand there, silhouettes against the golden evening light. It feels like a scene from my past—just like when we first met. Only then, I wasn't in love with one of them. Now, the weight of that love hangs in the air, thick with possibility and uncertainty.

My mind races as I navigate the winding roads back to my small apartment. Zayne's words echo in my head, mingling with the memories of my past. I'm torn between the life I've built here and the pull of the world I left behind. I replay the look in Zayne's eyes, the warmth of his embrace, and the promise of what could be.

Arriving at my apartment, I pull into the parking lot and turn off the engine. I sit there for a moment, the silence wrapping around me like a blanket. My heart thrums with fear, and a flicker of hope. I realize that whatever decision I make, it's mine to own. I've come so far to reclaim my life, but the idea of sharing it with someone who understands my darkness and cherishes my light is tantalizing.

As I step out of the car, I take a deep breath, letting the cool evening air fill my lungs. I glance back at the road, where possibilities stretch ahead like the sunset fading into night. Tomorrow will bring clarity, one way or another.

And with that thought, I walk toward my front door, ready to face whatever comes next, heart open and hopeful, knowing that I am in control of my destiny.

Chapter 25

Zayne

I text Kendall, though now she goes by Rebecca, letting her know we're heading to the steakhouse for breakfast. I can almost picture her reading my message, her green eyes narrowing slightly in contemplation. She doesn't ask how I got her new number—though I'm sure the answer is obvious. Oliver pulled up all her information, and last night, Killian and I spent hours parked outside her new apartment, waiting to see if she would make a run for it. But she didn't.

As we pull into the parking lot of the restaurant, the air is thick with hopefulness and the faint aroma of sizzling bacon wafts from inside. A flash of green catches my eye, and I turn to see Kendall parking beside us. Her green Mustang shines in the morning sun, and my heart races at the sight of her. When she steps out of the car, her bright green eyes are focused on me, and for a moment, the world around us blurs.

I open my car door and wrap my arms around her. She sinks into me, letting out a soft sigh as she allows me to hold her close, the warmth of her body against mine igniting something deep inside me. It feels like coming home. We walk in together, Killian trailing behind us, and choose a secluded booth in the corner, where the sun spills in through the window, casting a golden glow around us.

As we eat, the conversation flows in small, tentative bursts. I catch glimpses of the woman I remember, but there's a hesitance in her demeanor that makes my heart ache. She doesn't say much, and I can't tell if she's nervous because we intimidate her or if her mind is already made up—that no matter what I say or do today, she'll still tell me to go home without her. The thought gnaws at me, but I push it aside, focusing on the warmth of her presence instead.

When we finish our meal, Killian heads back to our hotel room, leaving me with Kendall. I slide into the passenger seat of her Mustang, allowing her to take the wheel as we drive toward the coast. The familiar thrill of being near her ignites within me.

Minutes later, we pull up to Lake Michigan, the waves crashing against the shore with a soothing rhythm. The lake stretches out before us, shimmering under the bright morning sun, and I can't help but smile at the beauty of it all. We step out of the car, leaving it behind as we walk along the shoreline, the cool breeze tousling our hair.

"I've missed you," she says finally, her voice barely above a whisper as we stroll along the water's edge, the sound of waves crashing echoing around us.

"I miss you too," I tell her, the weight of my emotions spilling out. "I was destroyed when I went to your room that night and you were gone."

She glances at me, her expression a mixture of regret and sadness. "I'm sorry. I couldn't tell you goodbye or I'd never leave, and I had to."

The confession hits me hard, but I know I shouldn't push her. "If I promised that you could do anything you want, anything at all, would you come home with me?" I ask, holding my breath as I wait for her answer.

She sighs deeply, the sound mingling with the crashing waves. "I'm not sure."

I nod, understanding her uncertainty. "You've been good here though, right?"

"Yeah, I have. It's really nice here."

"It's beautiful, just like you." I pause, letting my words linger in the air. She looks up at me, her green eyes sparkling with emotion, and I pull her into my arms, feeling the familiar rush of warmth that comes from holding her close. I lean down, capturing her lips in a soft kiss, my heart racing as our mouths connect.

For a moment, everything else fades away—the world, the past, the uncertainty of the future. It's just us, lost in the kiss, the taste of her lingering on my lips as I pull away slightly, looking deep into her eyes. In that moment, I realize I would do anything to keep her in my life, to show her that she can have both freedom and love. But the question remains: will she take that leap with me?

"If I left the club, would you be with me?" The words escape my lips before I can second-guess myself, the weight of my question hanging in the air like a fragile promise. I feel a knot tighten in my stomach, knowing that if I were to leave my brothers behind, they might hate me for it. But the thought of a life without Kendall feels unbearable. I've never felt this way about anyone, and I can't let her slip away again.

A year apart from her was torture and as soon as Oliver found her, Killian and I headed straight here so I could see her. So I can try one last time to bring her home.

"Zayne, you can't," she replies, her voice trembling as she takes a step back, creating a distance between us that feels like a chasm.

"I can and I will if it means being with you." I reach out, gently pulling her chin up so that she looks me in the eyes. "I'd do anything for you." The sincerity in my voice is undeniable, and I can see a flicker of hope behind her fear.

"No, Zayne. You can't do this." She turns away, heading back to her car, and my heart sinks as I follow her. Once we're seated inside the confines of her vehicle, the weight of our emotions fills the air, thick and heavy. Suddenly, she starts crying, and the sight of her tears pierces my heart. "Why would you do that for me?" Her voice is soft, almost broken, as she wipes her eyes.

"Because I love you," I tell her, the truth pouring out of me with a force that leaves no room for doubt.

"But to leave what you built? That's insane." Her voice trembles, a mixture of disbelief and concern etched across her face.

"Maybe I'm a bit crazy for you, then," I reply, forcing a smile despite the turmoil swirling within me. Her sniffles cut through my heart, and I reach out, brushing my thumb against her cheek, wiping away a stray tear.

"I don't want you to lose everything for me," she says, her voice a whisper. "You have a life, a family."

"I can build a new life," I insist, my voice firm. "I'll find a way to make it work. With you. I don't want to just exist in this world—I want to live it with you by my side. I want us to create something beautiful together."

She looks away, grappling with her thoughts, and I can see the conflict in her eyes. "But what if it doesn't work out?"

"Then we'll figure it out together," I say, feeling a surge of determination. "I'm willing to take that risk because I believe in us. I believe in what we can be."

The silence hangs between us, thick with unspoken possibilities. I can see her heart battling with her mind, and I reach for her hand, intertwining our fingers, letting my warmth seep into her.

"Kendall, I want to be the man who makes you smile every day, who stands beside you through thick and thin. You make me better, and I need you in my life. Just say yes."

Her gaze finally meets mine, and in that moment, I can see her walls starting to crack. "Zayne…" she begins, but I squeeze her hand gently, urging her not to finish that sentence.

"Just think about it," I say softly. "You deserve to be happy, and I promise I'll do everything I can to make you feel safe and loved. I'll never try to control you or limit your freedom."

As the sun begins to rise higher in the sky, casting a warm glow through the windshield, I hold my breath, waiting for her answer. In the depths of her eyes, I see the spark of possibility, the flicker of hope that maybe, just maybe, she might say yes.

Chapter 26

Kendall

After spending some time at the lake, the gentle lull of the water still dancing in my mind, I find myself driving back to my apartment. The soft glow of the setting sun filters through the trees, casting dappled shadows on the road ahead. It's stupid to let him this close to me because I know it'll be that much harder to let him go. But being wrapped in Zayne's arms feels so good, like a warm, familiar blanket that I'm not ready to cast aside just yet.

As I step into my kitchen, I pour us each a glass of water, the sound of the liquid filling the glasses a soothing backdrop to the whirlwind of emotions I'm feeling. I hand him his glass, and he takes a sip, his eyes never leaving mine. Setting his glass down, he reaches for my hips, drawing me closer to him until there's barely any space left between us. My heart races as his mouth presses against mine, and I wrap my arms around his neck, letting him in.

"I need you," he whispers against my lips, the longing in his voice sending shivers down my spine. His hands find the hem of my shirt, tugging it off with a gentle insistence before trailing kisses along my neck and collarbone, igniting a fire within me.

Without thinking, I lead him to my room, a mix of excitement and apprehension coursing through me.

Together, we work to help each other undress, our movements becoming more frantic with every layer that falls away. Once we are both naked, I lay back on the soft sheets, feeling the cool fabric against my heated skin as he crawls over my body, a predatory grace in his movements.

Our mouths reconnect, the kiss deeper than it's ever been as he presses himself against me, his erection sliding against my wetness. A moan escapes my lips, filled with need and longing. "I love you," he whispers, his voice raw with desire as he thrusts into me slowly, filling me completely.

The sensation is overwhelming, a beautiful invasion, and I can't help but buck my hips in response. "I love you too," I cry out, the words spilling from my mouth like a prayer as he begins to slam into me repeatedly, the rhythm becoming frantic and desperate. His hands press down on the bed on either side of my head, holding himself up as he peppers kisses across my cheeks and lips, each touch igniting the tranquility easing between us.

I wrap my legs around his waist, pulling him deeper, urging him on as he nails me to the bed. The room is filled with the sounds of our shared pleasure—sweaty bodies gliding together, moans mingling in the air, creating a symphony of intimacy that I never want to end.

When my orgasm strikes, it hits me like a tidal wave, crashing over me in a euphoric rush. I scream out in pleasure, a heartbroken pain mingling with my bliss as the weight of reality crashes in—this will be the last time I ever see him, feel him, and I can't handle the emotional toll that comes with that thought.

He lifts my right leg over his waist, grinding deeper into me, pushing us both closer to the edge. The world around us blurs as we fly over the next release together, our bodies trembling in unison. I can feel him coming just after me, a warmth that spreads through my core and intertwines with my own. We collapse together, him pressed down onto me, the weight of his body a comforting presence as he kisses my lips, cheeks, and nose, each touch tender and lingering.

"Don't let this be the last time I ever see you," he begs as though he can read my mind, his voice thick with desperation.

Tears spill down my cheeks, a mixture of joy and sorrow, and I turn away, unable to face the reality of his words. He gently grabs my chin, forcing me to look at him. The intensity in his gaze makes my heart race.

"Kendall, please. I need you. I'll do anything for you."

Through my tears, I whisper, "I don't know what to do anymore. I want you, but I'm so scared of what comes with that." The vulnerability in my voice hangs in the air, a raw truth that exposes the depths of my turmoil. I want to dive into this love, to let go of my fears, but the weight of everything still looms large.

Zayne's expression softens, and I can see the determination in his eyes. "We can face it together. I'll fight for you, for us, no matter what it takes."

His words resonate deep within me, and for the first time, I start to believe that maybe, just maybe, I could find the courage to embrace what lies ahead.

So, against my better judgment and everything I promised myself, I nod as tears stream down my face, soaking his chest. The warmth of his skin is a comforting refuge as he hugs me tight, his heartbeat steady and reassuring beneath my ear.

"I promise that this will be the right thing," he whispers, his voice a low, soothing rumble that vibrates through me. "I promise to always love you and protect you."

As he lays beside me, pulling me into his strong arms, I feel a sense of safety envelop me. The scent of him—a mix of leather and something uniquely him—fills my senses, grounding me in this moment despite the confusion swirling in my mind.

"You better," I reply, my voice muffled as I wipe my eyes with the back of my hand, smearing the remnants of tears across my cheeks. "Or so help me, I'll go so far away you'll never find me." The threat hangs in the air, laced with a hint of playfulness, but my heart knows it's laced with truth as well.

He chuckles softly, the sound vibrating through his chest, and I can feel a smile tugging at the corners of my lips despite the heaviness in my heart. "I'd chase you to the ends of the earth, beautiful," he murmurs, his breath warm against my hair, igniting a flicker of hope within me.

In this cocoon of warmth and promise, I cling to him, letting the world outside fade away. The weight of our shared uncertainty feels lighter in this moment, and I dare to believe that maybe, just maybe, we can carve out a path forward together.

The next morning, Killian pulls up in his Camaro, its engine rumbling softly as I gather the last of my things, cramming what I can into my car. There's a quiet finality in the air, a mix of nerves and excitement that tugs at my chest. Killian will handle the rest to ease the stress on me, and I've left the bigger furniture behind, knowing Zayne has promised me anything I need or desire once we settle in Atlanta.

Yesterday was a blur of tangled sheets and whispered promises, Zayne and I wrapped up in each other until the lines between where he ended and I began disappeared. He took me with a tenderness I hadn't known before, over and over, each time building something deeper inside me. It was the first time I ever gave myself over so freely, so willingly. Though he's only the second person I've been with, it felt like the first time, the way Zayne made me feel cherished, like I was the only thing in his world that mattered. As night fell, we drifted off to sleep with me nestled against him, my promise to leave with him back to Atlanta hanging in the air like the start of a new chapter.

Now, standing outside my apartment, I cling to Zayne, feeling the cool morning breeze brush against my skin as Killian slams his trunk closed. The apartment is hollow, just like the life I'm leaving behind, but it's not sad—it's freeing. This place had been my sanctuary, my experiment in independence, but I know now it was never home.

"Meet you back at your place," Killian calls out, giving Zayne and me a knowing nod before climbing into his car and peeling away down the street to the office of the complex.

Zayne shifts beside me, his thumb brushing over my hand as he looks down at me, his eyes soft and filled with unspoken words. "Ready?" he asks, his voice low but full of certainty.

I take a deep breath and slip my Mustang keys into his hand, a symbol of closing one door to open another. "Yeah, I'm ready," I say, my voice steady, the truth of it settling in my bones.

Zayne smiles, that lopsided grin that makes my heart flutter, and opens the passenger door for me. As I slide into the seat, he circles around to the driver's side, the ease in his movements grounding me. With a soft roar, we pull out onto the street. I glance back only once at the place where I spent the last year learning what it meant to be on my own, where I found parts of myself I hadn't known existed, and where I realized that no matter how far I ran, Zayne was the piece I was missing.

I turn back to the road ahead, the sun climbing higher into the sky, casting a warm glow over everything. Zayne squeezes my hand, his fingers threading through mine as we weave through traffic, moving faster, moving forward. I smile, feeling the weight of the past lift, because I know now that this is where I belong. Beside him. With him. My avenging angel.

From The Author

Dear Reader,

Thank you so much for taking the time to read my story. I poured my heart into these pages, and knowing you've shared this journey with me means the world. Your support fuels my passion for storytelling, and I hope this book brought you joy, excitement, a thrill, or maybe even gave you a few moments of escape.

If you enjoyed the story (or even if you didn't), I'd love to hear your thoughts. Reviews are incredibly helpful for authors like me, and your feedback not only helps me grow but also helps other readers discover this book. Whether it's a few words or a detailed review, your voice matters.

Thank you again for being part of this journey. Until next time—happy reading!

With gratitude,

Tasia Timm

Authors Work

Binding Hearts Series:

Binding Hearts: Book One

Binding Hearts: Book Two

Where Do I Belong

**Bound By Love

**Troubled Love

Flesh & Flame Series:

Flesh & Flame

**TITLE TBA

The Avenging Angels Series:

The Crimson Knights

**TITLE TBA

**TITLE TBA

**To Be Released

Made in United States
North Haven, CT
17 February 2025

65926872R00114